I0612654

THE
COMPLEX
LIFE

Book One of THE COMPLEX TRILOGY

HEATHER HAYES

Published by AH Digital FX Studios, INC 08/24/2018
AH Digital FX Studios, INC
10551 E. Ririe Hwy.
Idaho Falls, ID 83401
www.ahfx.net

ISBN: 978-1-945597-06-0

Library of Congress Control Number: 2018956642

Cover by Adam Hayes
Book Layout & Design by Adam Hayes

For Mom and Dad Hayes
Thanks for including me in your family,
flaws and all.

Chapter 1

I CAN'T HEAR MYSELF THINK. The 30 girls around me are so excited that their voices have lost their distinctive words and have become a loud buzzing beehive around me. Well, that's what I've been told a beehive sounds like, anyway.

"Elira!"

Oh. I heard that. That's my name. I wish it wasn't coming from the owner of that annoying, bossy voice though.

I open the drawers under my bed and start pulling all my clothes out. I don't look up as I ask, "What do you want, Mara?"

Mara flicks her white-blonde hair at me with her shriveled hand. I flinch as it hits me in the eye. "Everyone else is packed and waiting for you. Hurry up or we'll leave you here and move into the glass dorm without you."

"Go ahead and try. Mentor Maxine won't leave any of us behind."

"Has your purple birthmark affected your brain? The glass dorm is the best dorm in the whole complex! You should be waiting at the door like the rest of us. You have five minutes, raccoon-face." Mara turns around and yells at the rest of my roommates, "Get your bags and line up in the common room. We're about to meet the boys, my friends!"

I walk across the room to the big mirror by the door. Girls bump me with their gray duffel bags as they rush out of our room. I finally have the mirror to myself. My reflection reveals that my green right eye is also red now. Mara's whip-like hair is to thank for that. My left eye is surrounded by a purplish birthmark that continues along my face and behind my left ear. I gently hide some of it behind my light-brown hair, then I give up and push my hair behind my ears. I rarely bother hiding my birthmark. I don't really care what the other girls think about my looks. We've lived together so long, we all know who's where on the prettiness pecking order. I've been told by my mentors that it looks like I have half a raccoon mask. I wouldn't know for sure, of course. I've never seen a raccoon or been outside since I was two.

Mentor Maxine pokes her head in and hangs up a brand-new calendar on the wall next to the mirror. It's January first.

The biggest day of the year. My dormmates and I have gone through this ritual many times; we move out of the dorm we've lived in all year and into a new dorm. The new dorm is always bigger and nicer than the last one. The glass dorm has an added benefit that we've all heard rumors about, and I think everyone, especially my best friend, Avra, is more excited about this move than usual. I am curious, but I didn't lose sleep over it last night. I'm excited to start new classes. I like that part. I like to learn new things.

I have lived in the complex for as long as I can remember. I am one of the lucky ones. It's very expensive to pay for a spot in the complex. The outside world has become toxic from hundreds of years of pollution and chemical warfare. It's so toxic that almost the entire human race is plagued with deformities.

I wonder if my parents are still alive sometimes. They must have given up everything to pay the fee for my spot inside the complex, while they suffer outside in the toxic environment. Avra says the toxins have surely killed them by now. What selfless people they must have been. I really am lucky.

I walk back to my bed and shove all my clean, size medium black, white, and gray jumpsuits into the two gray duffel bags that I own. Now my buttons. Ow! I accidentally prick my finger on the back of one of the round, yellow, metal buttons that I am required to wear. All seven of them fit perfectly in a little side pocket on my duffel bag. I wipe the drop of blood from my fingertip onto my black sock. I check to make sure my name, Elira 223, is embroidered on the bags. Since all 30 of us 16-year-old girls have the same gray duffel bags, the workers in textiles embroider our names on them so we don't mix them up. Last January, I accidentally packed my stuff into Avra's duffel bags. She didn't mind; she's awesome like that. I had to pick long, black, curly hair off my clothes after we switched dorms though. Avra's hair used to be beautiful, but it's getting thinner all the time. She wears a red button because she has internal deformities that affect her heart and cause hair loss.

The bossy voice from before interrupts my reminiscing. "Mentor Maxine is waiting. I only have one working hand, and I still packed in half the time you're taking," Mara snarls as she flips her hair again. I turn away to protect my eyes. A strand of her hair gets caught on the orange button pinned to her chest. She frowns as she drops her bags to untangle her hair with her good hand; she gets minimal assistance from her shriveled hand.

I throw the last pair of socks in my bag with a little bit more force than necessary. "I know, Mara. I'm done, I just have to zip up my bags. Now get out of my face!" I glare at her as I force the sides of my bag together, so it will zip.

Avra waits for Mara to stomp away before she slides up to the side of my narrow bed and helps me get my second bag zipped. "Please don't fight with Mara today of all days."

I look from Avra to Mara's smug face that is now leaving the room. "I won't. I just hate being bossed around." I finish zipping up my second duffel bag. "I don't want to ruin this day for anyone, especially you."

"Do you think real boys look like the boys in our school books?"

I stop and try to think if I have ever seen any boys when I've been to the doctor's office inside the confusing halls of the complex over the years. There are pictures and books with bodies of boys and girls in the doctor's office, but I'm sure I've never seen a boy in person. Both of the doctors I've seen are male, but they are old, so is the director of the complex. I've never seen a male who is under 40 years old. "Yeah, I'm sure they do. Why?"

"I really like the looks of the boy on page 91 of the science book. I wonder if any of the boys in the complex look like that."

"Maybe, we'll know in about ten minutes."

Avra picks her duffel bags up off her bed then sets them back down again. They are heavier than she can comfortably carry. "Elira, why don't they let us see the boys in the complex until we're 16?"

"I don't know."

Avra starts to wobble on her feet, "I feel like my heart is going to pound its way out of my chest."

I steady her with one hand. "Don't get yourself sent to the doctor's office. I will ask Mentor Maxine if she knows why, the next time she's in a talkative mood. I'm guessing it isn't necessary because we'll never share dorms and most of the jobs at the complex are done by all one sex or the other."

"Which of the jobs are done by both sexes?"

"I'm pretty sure gardeners, janitors, chemists, and artists are jobs done by both sexes. Why?"

Avra's head droops. "Really? I was hoping cooks were both."

I let go of my friend as her balance stabilizes. "Oh yeah, I think you're right. I think most cooks are female, but they have some male cooks. Somebody has to bring the boys their victuals every day."

Avra looks pleased. "Good."

I smile at her. "You will be making my victuals two years from now. Crazy."

"You always pay more attention to what the mentors say than I do."

"You're right. It wouldn't hurt you any to pay attention more. I'm ready. Let's go see this glass dorm!"

Avra giggles nervously, "Yay!"

I put one duffel bag over each shoulder and discreetly lift the back of one of Avra's bags as I follow her into the common room. I don't want her to overwork her heart or fall down with fatigue. A long line of teenage girls is glaring at us as we enter. Huh, it looks like I really am the last one. Oh well. The back of the line won't kill me.

Mentor Maxine's tall, thin form walks to the double doors of the dorm and unlocks them with a key that she slips into the pocket of her purple jumpsuit. She stands in front of the slightly open doors. "Ladies, may I have your attention please? I know you are all excited about this move compared to all the other January first moves you've made, but you must quiet down and use decorum. The glass dorm is special because the school room of this dorm has a thick glass window on one side. You will be able to see through the glass into the school room of the 16 boys dorm. There is a telephone on the glass wall that can be held to your ear and mouth. If someone on the other side of the glass wall picks up their telephone, you can talk to each other about the school work you're doing. Consulting people with different points of view about your studies can be very enlightening."

Liza, the girl in front of Avra snickers, "Yeah right! I'm going to talk to the boys about anything but schoolwork." She straightens her black jumpsuit and fluffs her red hair with a thumbless right hand.

Liza's friend Jade twirls her black hair around her finger. "I am going to find the best looking one for myself."

I scoff, "What's the point? He'll always be on his side of the glass, and you on yours."

Mentor Maxine clears her throat and continues, "Since there are 60 of you and 55 of them, the telephone requires a sign-up sheet to use. You will stay in this dorm for two years instead of one. This is the last dorm you will have with each other as an age group. There are already 30 girls in there who have lived in the glass dorm for the last year. You will learn from each other and prepare yourselves to accept a job when you turn 18. At that time, you will share a dorm with women of all ages who do the same job as you. Please straighten out your line and follow me into the next dorm over."

Avra turns toward me and giggles nervously as she squeezes my hand. I hope her heart can handle this. Maxine throws open the doors, and we follow her into the glass dorm in a rush of anticipation.

Chapter 2

OUR FEET SOUND LIKE THUNDER as we rush
through the double doors behind Mentor Maxine. So much for
keeping in a straight line. I cannot believe how big this dorm
is. Our last dorm was narrow and everything from the floors
to the ceiling was brown and wooden. The dorm before that
was floor to ceiling yellow plastic. This dorm is called the glass
dorm for good reason. Everything is white and covered in glass
sculptures and chandeliers as we walk into the common room.
A group of girls I've never met before is staring at us from their
seats on white chairs and sofas. We are invading their space.

Mentor Maxine clears her throat loudly to get our

attention. "As you can see, the tables and chairs you will eat your victuals at are directly behind me. Victuals will be delivered at 7:00, 12:00, and 5:00. Your bedrooms and bathrooms are to your left through those two sets of doors. The school room is to your right, down the hall and through the only door on the right. As usual, the sofas and chairs around you are for relaxation and socialization time. If you want them to stay white, keep your hands clean. When you have chosen your new bed and put your personal items away, you may explore your new dorm for the rest of the day."

"YAY!" The wild stampede of girls rushing to the doors with bedrooms behind them is deafening. Their bags are so bulky that a traffic jam forms in the two doorways. I can't help but laugh at how stupid they all look trying to shove their way through. Avra motions to me that she wants to join them. I think it would be better for her heart if we wait for the crowds to clear out. I, myself, am not in that big of a hurry. I plop down on a white couch next to a girl with incredibly short, dark-brown hair and most of an ear missing. Avra frowns at me as she stands behind us twisting her chocolatey brown hands together, too nervous to sit down.

I look at the brunette with piercing blue eyes and say, "Hi, I'm Elira. What's your name?"

The girl looks at Avra and her red button, then at my yellow button and half a raccoon mask before answering, "I'm

Julie. I'm in the yellow club too." She has a dismissive air about her that I don't like.

I notice Avra twisting her hands harder as I say, "Yellow club?"

"Yeah. I can still hear perfectly well out of my messed-up ear, so I'm a yellow, not an orange."

"Okay, good for you. I personally don't think the colors of our buttons matter much."

Julie looks at me in disbelief. "Surely even you have noticed that the yellow button people are the healthiest."

I think about that for a minute as I sneak a peek at Avra's frowning face. "We may be the healthiest, but we're certainly not the prettiest."

Julie sniggers at me, "You've got that right; your half mask is hideous."

What a... I don't have to take this. "It was nice to meet you too," I snarl as I grab my bags off the floor. I head to the right-side door to check out the bedrooms behind the wall with Avra right behind me.

"I hope all the older girls aren't that rude," Avra whispers to me as we peek into the four bedrooms. As always, the room on the right side of the hall, next to the right-side bathroom, is filled with the sickest girls. The laundry chute is always in the right-side bathroom, and sick girls go through a lot of laundry. As I look at the girls in the right-side bedroom, I recognize about half of the faces. It'll be fun to get to know the older girls, as long as they aren't like Julie. Almost all of the girls in this room have red buttons. A few of them have extreme physical deformities like missing legs or missing arms, which qualify them for orange buttons. I feel bad for them. This toxic world is horrible to some people's bodies.

When we were little kids, there used to be more extremely deformed girls who lived with us. Some of them couldn't talk or walk. Most of them went to the final doctor and never came back. I wonder sometimes about why they didn't come back. I've always assumed that they died while at the doctor's office. I haven't found the courage to ask Mentor Maxine about that yet.

I'll be in the same room for two years in this dorm. To be honest, I really don't want to hear the sickly reds getting up over and over again in the night, so I'm not staying in their room. I've spent enough years of my life staying with them. I'm just going to be selfish this year and choose a different room. The next room over has lots of orange buttons. It's pretty full. I recognize Deedee, Rose, and Lacey choosing beds next to each other. Well, it's hard not to recognize them since their heads are all much smaller than they should be. I watch Julie, the yellow button snob with short, dark brown hair, walk into the next room over with a sneer directed at me as she goes. I don't care who else is in that room. I don't want to be in there with her. The left-most room is next to the other bathroom, and it has a window! Hardly any rooms in the complex have windows. I want this room.

"This is the perfect room, Avra! Let's pick two beds by the window."

We are almost trampled to death as twelve girls storm out of the window room and down the hall. Avra follows me as I find four empty beds by the window.

A plump girl with long red hair and freckles clears her throat from next to the door, "Uh, I wouldn't sleep that close to the window if I were you."

I look at her incredulously, "Why not?"

The girl spins her orange button around and around with her extremely small, crooked fingers as she answers, "The toxins from outside can seep into the cracks around the window, and make you sicker than you already are."

I raise my eyebrows as I look over the small, thick-paned window. "I don't see any cracks. I'm willing to take that chance. I like looking outside."

The overly-concerned girl shakes her head at me. "You're crazy. When you wake up feeling nasty, you might want to move to a bed closer to the door."

"Okay, will do." I roll my eyes so only Avra can see as we unpack our clothes, putting them in the drawers under our beds. Avra bites her bottom lip to keep from smiling.

"Vanessa, let's go check out the new boys in the school room with everyone else," an unusually-tall blonde with a red button says to the overly-concerned red-head. That poor blonde girl looks like someone strapped her to a machine and stretched her. She is at least 6'3" tall and can't weigh much more than 100 pounds.

"Okay, Shasta, let's go," Vanessa says as she pulls her long hair back into a ponytail. The two friends bump into Mentor Maxine as they leave the bedroom.

Mentor Maxine walks straight across the room towards us and motions for Avra to sit down on her bed. She sits down next to her and puts two fingers on Avra's wrist to feel her pulse. Maxine's eyes fill with concern as she sets Avra's hand back down. "Dang. Are you sure you don't want to stay in the sick room on the other side of the hall, Avra? The mentors keep medical supplies and snacks in there. It may be helpful if you feel faintness coming on."

Avra's brown eyes crinkle as she frowns. "I feel fine, Mentor Maxine. Elira can help me if I have any problems."

I nod in agreement. "Yeah, I'll help her. She'll be fine here with me."

Mentor Maxine sighs as she writes something on her clipboard. "Okay, I'm only going along with this because I trust you to help your friend, Elira."

"You know me. I'm as trustworthy as they come. What does 'Dang' mean, by the way?"

"Oh, it's just a word I say when I'm frustrated. There are more vulgar words some mentors use when they are frustrated, but I choose not to."

I look through the window at the outside as Mentor

Maxine tends to Avra. The last window I remember having was in the green dorm. That was six years ago. I almost forgot how beautiful the sky is. The light blue above contrasts with the white snow on the ground and the thick barrier of deep-green pine trees that surround the complex. The branches sway back and forth in a beautiful rhythm. "Is there a big fan out there, blowing the tree branches, so they wiggle and dance, Mentor Maxine?"

Maxine stands up and joins me at the window. "No, Elira, there is wind out there blowing things around. Don't you remember reading about wind in science class?"

I feel like an idiot. "Oh, yeah. I remember now. I wish I could feel it for myself."

Maxine looks down at her feet.

I notice a guard outside walking toward the window. It spurs another question. "Can the complex guards feel the wind through those thick white suits at all?"

"No, they can't. The suits and helmets are too thick to feel anything from the environment."

I nod. "It has to be that way to keep them safe from the toxins out there, doesn't it?"

"Mmmhmmm. I need to check on the other fragile reds. I will see you two at victual time."

As Mentor Maxine leaves, Avra asks me, "Why do you like Mentor Maxine so much?"

"She and Mentor Roberta are the only mentors who have followed us up each year."

Avra raises her eyebrows. "So?"

"The mentors who stay with the same dorm room never try to get to know me, so I don't try to get to know them. Mentor Roberta is horrible, and Mentor Maxine is nice. I can't help but like her."

"She's nice, but she is doing her job. Sometimes I think you waste your friendship on her instead of using it on the other girls."

I roll my eyes. "We've lived together long enough for me to know that most of the girls our age are fluff-heads."

Avra laughs as she puts her clothes in her drawers.

I don't tell Avra, but I like to think that my mother was like Mentor Maxine. When I was six years old, Mentor Maxine started working at the complex. We were in the purple dorm that year; my best friend had been Heidi at that time. She had a large head and was getting sicker and sicker every day. We were playing with dolls on the floor beside our beds one day, when Heidi groaned and fell over sideways, stiff as a board. Tears streamed down my face as I screamed for help. This wasn't the first time a friend of mine had died. The mentors usually just took them away without much explanation. I always wanted more. What did I want exactly? Maybe comfort? Compassion? Empathy? A hug? Those things were hard to come by in the complex, that is, until Mentor Maxine started working here.

After Heidi's body was removed, Mentor Maxine picked me up off the floor and hugged me for a while. She told me, "It is okay to be sad and cry, Elira. It's a terrible thing to lose your best friend." She stroked my hair and wiped the tears off my cheeks. She introduced me to Avra that day and we have been best friends ever since.

Avra wakes me up out of my daydream. "Let's go to the school room! I can't wait to see a boy!"

I really can't blame her. I want to see them too. "Yes! Let's go see these mysterious boys."

Chapter 3

THE SCHOOL ROOM IS HUGE. Sixty white desks are lined up in the middle of the room. Whiteboards line the front, and experiment stations line the sides. It's hard to focus on those things though, with the top half of the back wall acting as a giant window into an equally-huge school room full of boys!

My mouth drops open as I stand there in awe. At least 40 boys of different colors, shapes, and sizes are looking through the glass at us. Some of them are pressing their foreheads and noses against the window, some of them are standing back a couple of feet, but all of them are looking at us as wide-eyed as we are at them.

I shake my head in amazement. "I can't believe all of these boys have lived on the other side of the complex our whole lives."

Avra starts to wobble on her feet. I grab her and set her in one of the white desks. She turns around so she can keep staring at the boys. "Elira, some of them are better looking than the boy in the science book." I nod, still shocked at what these boys are making me feel inside.

The telephone is being used by a pretty, brunette girl with only one foot and an orange button. The boy on the other side has a yellow button and is tall with most of his chin missing. They are laughing and smiling at each other. The line for the telephone is as long as the classroom. I hear a beeping sound as the next girl in line says, "Time's up. My turn." The pretty brunette girl presses her hand to the glass, and the boy on the other side presses his hand on the glass on his side. They seem to be struggling to leave each other. Even after they hand the phones off, they walk, or in her case hop, with their hands pressed to the glass, sliding to the other end of the glass wall, bumping into people as they go.

I feel something weird stirring inside of me as I watch them. I remember having a brief lesson about this natural desire for females and males to be together in science class. I never really understood it until now. The pull we're all feeling toward these new and exotic boys is strong enough that I bet if I offered any of the girls my dessert for a month if they left the school room right now, none of them would take me up on it.

Some of the boys are surprisingly pleasant to look at. My eyes keep wandering back to the same few. I wonder what their voices sound like. Some of the boys are not attractive at all. One of the unattractive ones is puckering his lips at Mara as she flicks her white-blonde hair and laughs. Ew, that sight makes my stomach turn. Some of the boys are hyperactive and seem to annoy the other boys. One in particular, with curly-blonde hair and a red button keeps tipping people's desks over when they aren't looking. Curly is irritating me, and I don't even live on that side of the glass.

One of the taller, nicer looking boys with black, spikey hair, light-brown skin, and lumpy scars all over his neck is writing something on a piece of paper at a desk. He walks up to the glass and presses the paper to it. I jump out of my seat before I realize what I'm doing to get close enough to read it.

I'm Scott 194. I want to know the girl's name who is sitting at a desk with brown skin, black hair, and a red button.

My eyes fill with excitement as I race back to Avra to tell her what the boy's message says. She looks like she might collapse onto the floor. I find a discarded piece of paper at an experiment station and a marker on the floor and watch Avra write a message back telling Scott her name. I can't help but feel jealous as she walks up to the glass wall and presses the paper to it. She is wobbly enough that I join her at the glass just in

21

case. Scott smiles at her and presses his hand to the glass. Avra is much shorter than Scott. She has to reach high to place her hand on his. Just then, Mentor Roberta's short figure marches into the room.

"Okay, that's enough flirting. The victuals are on the tables; everybody go eat." When no one moves, she pulls a small box out of her wide, purple jumpsuit pocket and pushes a button. A loud shrill noise blasts into my ears. "I won't warn you again. Go eat your victuals." The loud noise fills the air yet again. Cruel woman. Girls hustle out of the room in droves now. Anything is better than hearing that again. Avra waves at Scott and starts walking away. She slips a little bit. Mentor Roberta runs to her and helps her stand up straight. "Are you okay, Avra?"

"Yes, I'm fine. My heart is just a little fluttery today."

Mentor Roberta sneers and writes something on her clipboard. "I'm sure it is. That's why we don't let you see the boys until now; your hearts can't handle it." Then almost as an afterthought she mutters, "Neither can your work ethic."

I try to figure out what Mentor Roberta means as we shuffle down the hall to the common room.

The tables are full except for two spots at a sickly red table. Avra and I sit down with the red-button girls and peel back the aluminum foil from our trays. The victuals look delicious. I love how new dorms mean new food too! My tray has a mound of vanilla pudding in one corner, a golden-brown chicken breast, buttery potato cubes, a brown roll, and what looks like little green trees. I stab one with my fork and sniff it. It doesn't have a very strong scent. I place it in my mouth and bite down on the little branches. It is buttery and plant-flavored. I kind of like it.

A sickly girl across the table who's laying on one arm says, "It's called broccoli. We get it every other day in the glass dorm."

Julie, the mean girl I met today, leans her chair back so she can speak into my ear, "You like to sit with the best of the best, don't you?"

I push her chair back down to the ground and away from me. "Turn around and shut up, Julie."

"I can tell you are going to be a delight to share a dorm with," she hisses back.

I turn my chair so I can ignore her better. I look across the table at the sickly girl who explained broccoli to me and smile at her. "I've never heard of broccoli before. I like new food. I'm Elira. What's your name?"

The girl sits up straighter. Her eyes keep rolling back in her head. "I-I-I'm Gr-Gr-Gretta. I want to be a gardener someday. I like to study plants."

"Huh, that's neat. Uh, you don't look very good. Do you feel okay?"

"I-I don't know why it keeps going dark..." The girl barely finishes her sentence before falling face first into her tray. She stops moving. I jump up and pull her out of her food. Her eyes are closed, and vanilla pudding is sliding down her cheek onto her chest. She doesn't seem to be breathing.

I scream as I shake Gretta, "Mentor Roberta! Come quick!"

Avra, Julie, and the other girls around me are frozen in their seats as they watch Mentor Roberta rush over to us and check Gretta for breathing and a pulse. She doesn't find one. She pulls the little communication box out of her pocket and turns a dial. She speaks into the box, "I have a defunct one in the female glass common room, 151 red."

I want to scream at Mentor Roberta. I pound the table with my fist and then start smacking Gretta's cheeks with my hand. Maybe I can slap her back to life. I stop as the soft flesh of her face turns hard. Why isn't Mentor Roberta trying to save her? Why is she talking about this nice person like she's just a number on her clipboard?

Mentor Roberta shakes her head at me and forces me back to my seat. She stands straighter and clears her throat. "I hope you all feel grateful right now. You are incredibly lucky to be inside the complex away from the deadly toxins that kill people outside. This poor red had more internal deformities than our complex could save her from. The outside world is nothing but everyday death. Be grateful you live in the complex with only occasional death." Julie nods her head then digs into her food. I slump in my seat and look at the broccoli on my tray, wishing Gretta could tell me more about it. I wish she could tell me anything at all. I feel tears leaking from my eyes as I lay my head on the table. I can't look at her still form a minute longer.

Three mentors burst through the door. They take Gretta away. They don't say anything more to us. It is like Gretta never existed.

Chapter 4

MOST OF THE GIRLS RUSH BACK into the school room after 12:00 victuals. I keep my head on the table until Mentor Roberta forces my head up with both of her hands. I'm sure a big rosy-red cheek stares back at her.

"You don't need any more splotches than you already have, Elira. Sit up."

I sit up, but my frown isn't going anywhere.

"Crying won't bring her back. You need to move so we can disinfect the table. Go to the school room with everyone else or go to bed."

Avra tugs on my sleeve and whispers, "Come on, Elira. Come to the school room with me."

I drag myself out of my seat and follow Avra to the school room. The rest of the girls have forgotten Gretta already and the flirtations have moved up a level. Mara has both hands on the glass with the ugly boy from before putting his hands on hers from the other side. They look like they're trying to figure out a way to kiss with four inches of glass between them. Gag.

My eyes are drawn to the same few boys as before, but then a new face captures my attention. He is tall with a broad shoulder, not shoulders, because one of his shoulders is missing as far as I can tell. The arm on that side lies shriveled and limp. The other side of him looks like it has taken up the slack. That arm is the most muscular one in the entire room. The boy's face is oval-shaped with a strong jaw. His hair is a dark red, kind of auburn color. His eyes are green just like mine. While the other boys are at the glass gawking at us, he is slinking around the room testing the strength of the items in the classroom. The scrawny mentor on their side is plenty busy watching the boys at the glass. Bicep, as I'm already calling him, takes the mentor's desk drawers out, one at a time, pulls on them to see if they will break apart, and then puts them back in.

He takes apart the door's hinges and then puts them back together before anyone notices. Then he gets gutsy and takes apart the sink at an experiment station. I'm afraid he's going to get caught as the skinny mentor stands up out of a student desk and stretches. A ghostly pale boy with black hair and an incredibly good-looking boy with dirty-blonde hair walk over to the boy in trouble and help him put the faucet back together as quickly as they can. I look across the room at the mentor to see if he's noticed, but he is talking to, wait, the good-looking boy with dirty-blonde hair? How did he get over there so fast? I look back at the sink, but Bicep and the black-haired guy are the only ones there. They slurp water out of the sink that is in fine working order again. Wait, do I see someone laying on their back inside the sink cabinet? I look back at the mentor; the good-looking guy is still there talking to him. That guy did some crazy fast moving. I wonder how I missed it.

Boom, boom, boom. My eyes are forced to a line of boys pounding on the glass wall in a steady rhythm with their eyes bulging and their jaws hanging open. What are they looking at? I look at a group of girls to the left of me just in time to see Jade, the boy-crazy girl my age, pull the zipper on her jumpsuit down to just above her belly button. Her fingers grasp each side of the opening when Mentor Roberta pushes past me with her finger on the shriek button. We all cover our ears as Jade pulls her zipper back up. She is a few seconds too late. Mentor Roberta grabs both of Jade's shoulders and escorts her from the room at a steady march.

We girls all stare at each other wide-eyed and shocked at what just happened. What was Jade thinking? Mentor Roberta appears again somewhat out of breath.

"And that is how you lose your free time. There will be no evening free time in the school room after evening victuals for three months. If any of you try to pull a stunt like that again, there will be no evening free time for the rest of the year." Whines and moans permeate the air.

"That's not fair, Mentor Roberta. We never had a girl dumb enough to expose herself last year. We older girls shouldn't be punished for the stupidity of these brand-new younger girls," Julie insists.

Mentor Roberta tries to put a loose strand of gray hair back into her bun. "If you think that's not fair, just imagine the punishment you all would have received if I'd shown up one minute later. This punishment is nonnegotiable. If you see a fellow dormmate doing something stupid, stop her before you all pay the consequences."

We all unenthusiastically mutter, "Yes, Mentor Roberta."

"Jade will be detained for a few days, so don't expect to see her any time soon."

Vanessa, the overly concerned red-head from my room, raises her hand and asks, "Is she being charged as a dissident?"

Mentor Roberta laughs humorlessly. "No, if that's what you think dissidents do, then you have very little chance of becoming one yourself. Your evening victuals are ready. Go eat, but do not come back to this room after. If you do, you will find yourself in the same place as Jade."

As we all slink silently into the common room, Avra

points to a table with several other familiar faces our age. We watch Mentor Roberta unlock the door to the hall and slip out. As soon as the door clicks shut, the room erupts into chatter.

"What on earth did Jade think she was doing?" Avra asks Kimberly, a girl we've grown up with who has an enormous mane of golden ringlets and a missing chunk of cheek and nose.

Kimberly fluffs her golden mane. "Three boys asked her to do it. What would you have done?" The other girls at our table shrug their shoulders.

A sardonic laugh escapes my lips. "Of course I wouldn't do it, Kimberly."

Kimberly doesn't look like she believes me. "We've never had rules about things like that. If I'd been Jade, I would have been confused too."

A girl from the next table over leans her chair back and says, "She didn't look confused to me." Avra nods her head in agreement.

I look right at Kimberly. "We don't need to have rules about something to use our brains."

She glares at me, picks up her tray, and moves to another table. The other girls at our table follow her. Avra scowls at me. "How are we ever going to have friends if you insult everyone?"

"I can't pretend that these fluff heads aren't idiots. Please don't tell me you would do the same thing if Scott asked you."

Avra pauses for a second. My jaw drops. Please don't tell me my best friend thinks she should do what a stranger asks

31

without question. Thankfully, she shakes her head. "I wouldn't expose myself. I won't even change my clothes in front of other girls."

"Good." We eat our food alone and silently think about what just happened. The room is too loud to hear each other anyway.

Avra is extremely disappointed that she won't get to see Scott again tonight. She and I go into our room to escape the loud chatter about the boys and the punishment that we will all suffer from. Avra talks about Scott until she falls asleep. I think the excitement of the day wore her out.

As the world gets dark and drowsy, I enjoy my new bed by the window. The foot of my bed is pressed up against it. If I kneel on the end of my bed, I can look outside. I watch the wind in the trees, loving every minute I can get. I even see a bird in the trees as the sun sets. I wonder if the bird has a nest with eggs in it out there somewhere. I see a guard marching toward me. He is slow-moving and probably tired. I'm glad there is an outside light on this side of the complex. He leans against the building. I wonder if he's asleep behind that thick helmet...

Low branches wiggle on the pine trees straight across from me. I hope it's a raccoon or a fox! I would love to see a real animal like that. Huh, it doesn't look like any animal I've studied at school. What has long, black, curly hair in the animal kingdom? The only mammal I can think of is humans... An actual woman crawls on her hands and knees through the thick trees. How is she surviving the toxins? Or the snow that I've been told is very cold? She stands up and I can't visibly see any deformities on her pale white face, but her coat and gloves are covering most of her. Her deformities are probably internal. She starts walking—straight toward... me!

I don't know what to do, so I just stay where I am and watch. The woman moves her arms and hands in a quick, purposeful way. I think she's trying to communicate with me, but I have no idea what she is saying. She points at the guard who still seems asleep, and then she points to me and starts moving her fingers in intricate ways. I really wish I could communicate back, but I don't know how. I shrug my shoulders. Just then, the guard wakes up and runs toward the woman. She turns and runs back to the trees, crouches down, slips through the gap at the bottom of the trees, and is gone. The guard pulls a little communication box out of his protective suit and starts talking to someone.

"What are you looking at?" a deep female voice asks behind me. I turn around to see Mentor Roberta leering at me. I have never liked Mentor Roberta. She reminds me of the evil step-mother from the book Cinderella. She assists in keeping me alive, but she doesn't love, or even like me.

"I saw a grown woman crawl through a gap in the trees, but the guard chased her away. She didn't look like she had any deformities. How can that be?"

Mentor Roberta rolls her eyes and smirks at me. "Surely

you know by now that some deformities are on the inside, right?"

"Yes. I know. Why does she live out there? It's toxic."

"She can't afford a place in here, so she has no choice. The guards usually do a better job of keeping the riff-raff away from the complex. I will have to report this. Excuse me," Mentor Roberta says as she turns around and leaves.

Chapter 5

I HAVE WEIRD DREAMS THAT NIGHT about the mysterious woman in the trees. She knocks out the complex guard with a giant club and then tries to break my window with it. I wake up feeling unrested and full of questions. I eat my morning victuals in a daze. Julie bumps into me as I walk into the school room. Just great. I need to pay attention to what I'm doing.

"Watch where you're going, raccoon face."

"Oh, sorry. I don't want you to take away my membership to the yellow club. I'll watch out next time."

Julies eyes narrow. "You are so full of yourself."

"Yeah, that would be *me* you're talking about," I mumble as I shuffle to a desk next to Avra. I realize I don't have any paper, so I get up and approach the mentor's desk at the front of the school room. "May I have a piece of..." The grouchy look I get from the new school mentor makes me shut my mouth and take the piece of paper she extends toward me. I turn around and find my desk quickly.

This new school mentor is very tall which is intimidating to me. She is slightly curvy and has curly medium-brown hair that sits on top of her shoulders. Her black eyes stare out at us like cannon balls about to destroy us. Why can't they all be more like Mentor Maxine? She doesn't answer every question I have, but she's kind and cares about my development. I turn around and see the cute boy with dirty-blonde hair and blue eyes talking to his mentor from the second row of their school room. Avra nudges me so I turn around.

I'm not expecting a good experience as our new, grouchy mentor clears her throat. "Hello, my name is Mentor Bridget. I will be the mentor who prepares you for the jobs you will soon have. We will be adding chemistry and advanced algebra to your curriculum this year. Let's begin." She is stern, but she is very knowledgeable. I am surprised at how much I learn from her first lesson. I get my reading assignment done quickly. As I wait for everyone else to finish so we can move on to math, my mind wanders...

I wonder where the mentors sleep. They get days off, so

they have to go somewhere. I wish we were allowed to explore the complex. Unfortunately, the last girl who tried to leave her dorm through the doors the mentors use was charged as a dissident, and she never came back. I've wondered about some of these things for the past few years but seeing that normal looking woman outside makes it hard to think about anything else today.

Mentor Bridget has an approach to math that is very easy to understand. This crabby woman actually has skills. I finish this assignment quickly too. Mentor Bridget notices that I have nothing to do, and that my head keeps turning around to look into the boys' school room, so she writes an extra credit problem on the board. It looks like a fun challenge, so I get to work on it.

I'm glad the glass wall is in the back; it's distracting to know there are boys back there who could be looking at me. I sneak a quick peek behind me. The handsome boy with dirty-blonde hair is sitting on the back row now, near the glass wall. Wait, do their mentors let them change seats in the middle of lessons? He peeks at the same time I do. I look away quickly. My heart beats faster.

Luckily, their desks face the other way too. When we get exploration time, the telephone will be all abuzz I'm sure. I won't get to use it. Oh well. Avra will need help with today's assignment. She's not very good with numbers. She will need to figure it out if she wants to be a cook though. Cooks have to have at least a B average in math to get the job. No one wants the wrong number of ingredients put into the victuals.

I wonder what job I should apply for in two years. I am pretty good at all the school subjects. Mentor Maxine says I should be a chemist. I kind of like the thought of making things out of chemicals. But secretly, I want to know that I'm making a big impact on this crazy world of ours. How impactful will I be if I spend all day making soaps and cleaners for the janitors?

When Mentor Bridget's done teaching, she says, "You have 30 minutes of exploration time before victuals. Remember to sign up if you want to use the telephone." A mob of girls jump up and run to it.

Avra leans over to me. "Will you sign me up, please? I want to talk to Scott."

I roll my eyes and walk over to the sign-up sheet which is actually part of the glass wall. The line is long, but I wait patiently. I read all the girl names on the list already—what do you know, all the boy-crazy girls are on here. Reading the names of the boys is tricky. I have to read their names backwards since they wrote on their side of the glass. I use a marker to write 'Avra' on the glass on spot 25. On the boy's side of spot 25, I write Scott's name. I almost walk away, but then I decide to write my name on spot 26. I leave the boy side of spot 26 blank. If someone wants to talk to me, here's their chance. I doubt anyone does, but I do kind of want to hear what a boy's voice sounds like.

The marker in my hand is pulled out by some pushy girl behind me. The rush of girls crowding around the glass smooshes me against its cold, hard surface. Ah, back off people! I hope that I get my turn today, but since we lost our evening free time, it looks like it will probably be tomorrow or the next day. Oh well.

I sit down and ask Avra if she needs help with her math. I'm surprised to see that she is almost done with her assignment. "I like Mentor Bridget. She explains how to do the problems in a way that I can understand."

"Good, because I get tired of being your second teacher."

"Do you really?"

I smile at Avra as I pick a few curly stands of hair off her back. "No. I don't mind. Are you going to try the extra credit problem?"

"No, I want to see if I can find Scott when I'm done."

"Okay, but don't fall in love with him."

Avra lets out a breathless sigh. "I won't."

I have some serious doubts that Avra won't fall in love. She's easily captivated. I get back to my extra credit problem. It takes a while to get it done. I like it when mentors challenge me. This problem has me second guessing myself. I am pretty sure I am right though.

I stand up and look around the room. "Did anyone do the extra credit problem?" I yell out to the loud, giggling room. No

HEATHER HAYES

one answers back. They are too busy oogling the boys to do
anything extra today. Dang.

I look through the glass at the boy's school room. The
same extra credit problem is written on their white board. All
but five boys are turned around in their seats, or are standing
up to flirt with the girls through the glass. The five seated boys
are working on the extra credit problem. Mentor Maxine did
say that we should learn from other points of view. I wonder
if I can get one of the studious boys to look up. I walk over to
the telephone where flirty red-headed Liza is talking with a boy
who is missing an eye. I know the eye is missing because he flips
his black eye patch up as I approach the glass. Ahh! I can't unsee
that. Liza must like him for his dazzling smile because, ew.

"Hey, Liza, ask him if anyone on his side has finished the
extra credit problem." Surprisingly, Liza and the pirate boy help
me out.

I see the five heads leaning over their desks look up and
turn around. The good-looking, dirty-blonde-haired boy is
one of them. In fact, most of these faces look familiar to me. I
squeeze into the crowd at the window and press my paper to
the glass. The boy with black, curly hair and pale-white skin
from yesterday's sink escapade jumps up with his paper and
looks intently at mine. He looks at his own assignment and then
looks at mine again. He starts to nod. He mouths the words,
"You're right." He then presses his paper to the glass. I see that
on the top of his paper it says, *Rocky 173*. He solved the problem

exactly the same way I did. Awesome, I guess that's all I need...
but before I can get away from the glass, Rocky motions for the
other four problem-solving boys to join us.

Bicep is one of them. I'm thrilled to see that the good-
looking, dirty-blonde haired boy is one of them, and wait, here
he is again? Oh, he's actually a twin! Okay, that explains how I
saw him in two places at once. Identical thin faces with dirty-
blonde hair and blue eyes look back at me. They are about two
inches taller than I am, and I'm pretty tall, about 5'9. I can look
right into their eyes, and they are gorgeous. The only way I can
tell the boys apart is that one of them has a yellow button and
one of them has an orange button. A round-faced boy with a
shaved head looks at my paper and nods. He writes on the back
of his assignment, *Hey, beautiful, I'm Bryon. What's your name?*

My eyes pop open in surprise, and my cheeks feel like
they are on fire. I almost back away from the glass, but I
don't. I feel incredibly shy as the five faces look at me. They
stare at my raccoon eye, with curiosity. It makes me feel self-
conscious about my looks for the first time in many years. My
hand automatically pulls a chunk of hair forward to cover my
birthmark. Should I tell them my name, or am I just a freak
show to them?

After some deliberation, I decide that if these are the only
boys who do the extra credit, then I may as well know their
names for the next time I need help. I flip my assignment over
and write *Elira*. When I press the paper to the glass, I watch the

five boys' mouths try to sound out my name. One of the dirty-blonde haired boys writes on the back of his paper, *Is your name pronounced El - ih - rah, or Eel - ira?*

El - eye - ruh, I write back. The twins and Rocky smile and nod. Bicep nods and writes his name on Rocky's paper. His name is Andric. He'll always be Bicep to me though. The shaved-head boy, Bryon, winks at me then wrinkles his forehead and keeps trying to sound my name out. I've always known my name is a little weird, but I still like it. It's the only thing my parents gave me that I still have.

I point at the twins and shrug my shoulders. I hope they get what I mean. They both smile at the same time in a heart-stopping way and write on their papers. The papers pressed to the glass reveal that the twin with the yellow button is Jefrey. The twin with the orange button is Garth. I feel my cheeks turning red again as I look at them and nod.

Mentor Bridget interrupts my reverie as she taps me on the shoulder. "Elira, may I see your assignment please?" I hand over my assignment. Mentor Bridget looks at both sides of the paper before writing something down on her clipboard. "Very good, Elira. I'm glad we have at least one girl in this class with brains." She turns around and pushes the button on her square device that lets out a loud shrieky noise. "Victuals are ready; everyone clear the school room immediately."

I turn and see that the same thing is happening on the boy side. I wave at the five smart boys and gather up my things to walk with Avra to the eating area. I look back one last time before leaving the school room, I see Andric swipe a metal ruler off their mentor's desk. That boy is a trouble maker. Most importantly though, I see one of the twins looking back at me. I just can't tell which one.

Chapter 6

AS AVRA AND I GET READY FOR BED, I look outside our bedroom window. The guard is there, leaning against the building as usual. I see a glint of something in the trees; it looks like eyes. I wonder if it's that woman again. Upon closer inspection, a furry body and triangle ears poke out of the gap in the trees. Ooh, a fox. It's too dark to see the distinct orange color of the fur, but the white tipped tail gives it away. He's so cute! I press my forehead to the cold glass, completely fascinated. The fox suddenly disappears. I can't hear anything, but I'm pretty sure the guard has just shot at the fox. He has his gun out, and the fox is gone in the blink of an eye. I turn around to see Shasta, my tall, skinny, blonde roommate, looking over my head out the window.

"If I weren't a red, I would apply to be a guard."

I am shocked to hear this from such a shy, scrawny girl. I try to be funny. "Are you sure they make giraffe-sized guard suits?"

Shasta doesn't laugh.

I feel like a jerk. "I'm sorry, Shasta. I shouldn't have said that. I hate it when people make fun of my deformity too."

"It's okay. I'm used to it."

I think back to what she first said. "I didn't know that we could apply to be guards. I thought only mentors could do that."

"No, yellows can be guards, and a few oranges can. Not many girls get accepted as guards though, and reds are never accepted." Shasta looks down at the red button pinned to her chest with sadness in her eyes.

I look down at my own yellow button and tap it with my fingernail. I could be a guard. I have never considered that. "Shasta, would you feel comfortable shooting a gun?"

Shasta looks down at her long slender fingers. "Yeah, I think so. I like to protect the people I care about."

"I never would have guessed that about you. You seem so timid."

Shasta's face turns hard. "Even timid people can be protective."

Avra pipes in from under her covers, "I'm going to be a

cook." She lazily looks at the ceiling. "I like food, and I want to feed people. Reds can be cooks. Maybe we could be cooks together, Shasta."

Shasta smiles half-heartedly. "Yeah, maybe." She turns around and heads to her own bed. I watch to see if her feet hang over the edge of it. Yep. They do. That must stink.

"You're lucky, Elira," Avra says. "You could do any of the 12 jobs. You're smart, you're healthy, and you're a yellow. What do you want to do?"

I look outside and swear that I can see eyes peeking through the gap in the trees again. "I don't know. I keep changing my mind about what I want..."

TODAY MENTOR BRIDGET ANNOUNCES that the older 17 girls will be visiting their number one choice of job to see if it is a good fit for them. I'm okay with that, because it means less noise in the school room all day. The older girls line up and leave the school room with an elderly mentor I don't know. It's so quiet in here. I do my assignments plus several extra credit problems quickly without interruptions.

Once we're mostly done with our math, Mentor Bridget asks, "Since half of the class is trying out jobs today and we have some extra time, I would like to have a discussion about your futures with you. Who knows what the 12 complex jobs are?"

Mara flips her white-blonde hair up in the air as her hand reaches into the sky. "I do. They are: gardening, textiles, janitorial, chemistry, artistry, weaving, metal welding, cooking, guarding, laundry, fabrication, and carpentry."

"Correct. Can everyone do every job?"

Avra's hand shoots up. "No. Reds can only do gardening, janitorial, artistry, cooking and laundry."

"Correct. Can girls do every job?"

Mara the know-it-all pipes in again, "No. Girls can't do metal welding, fabrication, guarding, and carpentry."

"Incorrect. Girls can be guards. You must be both physically and mentally strong though. Out of the 20 guards we have at the complex, only two of them are female."

Liza giggles as she raises her hand to ask, "Which of the jobs can both sexes work together?"

Mentor Bridget narrows her eyes at Liza as she answers, "Quite a few actually: gardening, janitorial, chemistry, artistry, weaving, cooking, and guarding. But don't think that you can apply for a job just so you can flirt with boys the whole time. That just won't happen. Sorry."

Liza doesn't look deterred. "I'm going to get John to be a weaver with me," she whispers to Jade who is back from her punishment.

"Start thinking about the jobs you are interested in doing. These will be jobs you do for the rest of your lives, so pick carefully. I can help tailor your education to benefit you in your job. Just let me know what you are interested in. Exploration starts now. Make sure you get your assignments done and turned in before you approach the glass wall."

I am deep in thought about the freedom that guards must have to wander around the outside when I feel a tap on my shoulder. I turn around to see Vanessa, my roommate who's scared of windows, pointing to the glass wall. The five boys from yesterday are beckoning me to join them at the glass. I grab my paper and join them at the window. Both twins smile at me, and my heart starts beating a little bit faster. All four boys are wearing black jump suits. I wish the twins would wear different colors so I can tell them apart easier. Bryon winks at me, makes a heart with his hands and holds it in front of his real heart, and then moves it out and back like a heartbeat. Ugh. Rocky is smiling and pointing to his paper. I look at his extra credit problem and see that he has the same answer as me.

I nod my head and mouth, "I got that answer too."

He shakes his head and points to the writing in the corner of the paper. I read it, *Do you think that the mentors sleep here, in the complex?*

I frown and write, *I don't know, no one tells me anything about adult life around here. What do you know?*

Rocky wrinkles his forehead and writes, *I know that Mentor Bob doesn't sleep here. I overheard him talking to Mentor Jim about being tired and leaving this imaginary world to go home.*

This information bothers me a bit, but surely there is an

49

explanation. I write, *I'm pretty sure that there are other complexes. Our complex can't hold all the healthy people of the world. I will ask Mentor Maxine today. Sometimes I can get a little bit of information out of her.*

Rocky nods at me. *You do that, and we'll talk again tomorrow.*

I'm trying to understand why we aren't talking about school work. I write on my paper, *Why do you care?*

Rocky takes his time writing back, *I like to know what is really going on around here. I know that we are kept in the dark about a lot of things. For example, I know that there are people outside who aren't dying from toxins.*

I gulp. *How do you know that?*

Garth, the twin with the orange button writes on his paper, *We had a window in our bedroom last dorm, and we saw two healthy-looking people out there without suits.*

This information excites me. I write back, *I have a window right now! I've seen a woman out there. I've wondered why she looks so healthy. It is likely that she has internal deformities though.*

Jefrey smiles at me with those crystal blue eyes of his. He writes on his paper, *I knew you were smart.*

My cheeks heat up, heh, heh, how do I respond to that? I'll just change directions. *Why do you want me, of all people, to help you find out about the mentors' world, Rocky?*

You are the only girl over there who is wide-awake.

I look around my school room before I write, *Uh, everyone except Tessa, over there, is wide-awake in this room.*

Nope, you're the only one.

I have no idea what he is talking about. I watch Liza and Kimberly giggle next to me as they watch Curly put a garbage can on the skinny mentor's head. Now that I think about it, I do wonder about things and ask more questions than most girls. Is that what he's talking about? Mentor Bridget presses her loud alarm button just then. "Time for victuals, ladies. The last one in the school room has to clean the whiteboards." The room clears out in a hurry. I look back as I leave, and once again, one of the twins looks back and smiles at me. I wish I could tell which one.

Chapter 7

WHEN THE 17 GIRLS GET BACK to the dorm after
their day at potential jobs, I am clamoring to talk to anyone
who will acknowledge me. I sit at a table full of older girls.
"Vanessa, what job did you do today?"

Vanessa frowns at me suspiciously. "Why do you care?"

I pull the foil off my victual tray. "I'm a curious person, and
I know you have many skills to choose from. *Cough, cough.*"

Vanessa pulls the foil off her tray too and digs in like it's
her last meal. "I worked in textiles. I sewed 10 shirts and 10
skirts on an actual sewing machine today."

Huh, skirts. We all wear jumpsuits in the complex, even

the mentors. I look at Vanessa curiously. "I've seen those kinds of clothes in our textbooks, but, who wears them?"

Vanessa pauses for a second before shoveling a spoonful of chocolate pudding in her mouth. "I don't know. Maybe we get to wear different things once we get our jobs."

I nod, thankful for a logical explanation. "Yeah, that must be it. Did the workers in textiles wear shirts and skirts?"

Vanessa scratches her head with the handle of her funny squarish spoon. "No. They didn't. They must be for other jobs. Do you want your pudding? I'm starving."

"Um, no. Take it." Vanessa scoops the pudding out of my tray greedily. I turn to Shasta, who is eating quietly on my other side. After our conversation at the window last night, I feel like she just might like me. We'll find out. "Did you decide to check out the kitchens, Shasta?"

Shasta's long fingers set her fork down. "Yeah. The mentors thought it would be the best thing for me."

"So, how was it?"

Shasta's thin face breaks out into a smile. "Surprisingly, it was great. I loved making delicious and pretty things to eat, more than I thought I would."

I smile encouragingly at her. "Did you make the chocolate pudding in the trays tonight?"

"No... I made the most delicate white cookies that I have ever seen. We decorated them with sweet creamy frosting.

They taught me how to swirl the frosting around to make it look like the flowers in our text books."

I watch Vanessa lick the last of my chocolate pudding from her spoon. "Huh, I wonder who gets to eat them if it isn't us."

Shasta's forehead crinkles with thought. "Yeah, I kind of wonder that too... We made hundreds of them. Maybe they were for the boys."

"That must be it. Those lucky, spoiled brats. I'm going to check on Avra. Have a good night, Shasta."

"I will. You too."

THE CRYING COMING FROM AVRA'S BED is pretty loud.

"Why do I have to have this deformity?" she moans. When she was brushing her hair this morning, a whole handful fell out. I tell her not to worry about it, but now that Scott is giving her some attention, she is very self-conscious about her looks.

When Mentor Maxine comes in to check Avra's pulse, like she always does, I corner her. "Is Avra going to be all right?"

"Yes, don't worry about her. I'll take care of her."

"Do you think she'll be able to be a cook like she wants to?"

Mentor Maxine doesn't look at me as she writes on her clipboard. "Um, that is probably the best job option for her.

Being on her feet all day will be hard, but I can arrange for a chair or stool in the kitchens for her."

I look across the room at Avra's tear streaked face. "Do you think she'll have a long life?"

Mentor Maxine pauses before she answers, "I will do my best to make it is as long and happy as it is possible to be."

She isn't being very talkative. "Are you happy, Mentor Maxine?"

That question seems to disorient her. She pushes her gray-streaked brown hair behind her ears. "Yes, I am."

"I just wondered. Sometimes I see sadness in your eyes. What makes you happy?"

Mentor Maxine's wrinkles around her blue eyes stand out as she forces a smile. "I feel like I am helping you girls to the best of my ability. I try to be an advocate for you with the administration, and that makes me happy."

"Do we need an advocate?"

A shadow passes behind Mentor Maxine's eyes. "Everyone needs an advocate in this life, but I think you sweet girls need one more than most."

I think of how cold and distant the administration is when they come to inspect the dorms twice a year. "Does the administration care about us?"

Maxine gives away more than she knows as her eyes darken. "I feel like I do more than them, sometimes."

I know I'm pushing my luck with all these questions, but I

have one more I need to ask. "Do you live here at the complex? Or do you leave the complex when your shift is done?"

Mentor Maxine looks down as she picks some strings off her jumpsuit. "I leave when my shift is done. I take the... proper precautions to get to my apartment. I know, that is a new word for you. An apartment is a safe place to live for adults. It's a complex of its own."

"Do you wear a suit like the guards do when you leave?"

Maxine shakes her head and turns to leave. "I think it's time for you to go to bed. I love your inquisitive mind, but that's enough for today. Goodnight, Elira."

"Goodnight, Mentor Maxine." Dang. I felt like I had her on a roll. Oh well, at least I can tell Rocky that I know mentors don't live here.

As I change into my pajama suit, I look out the window. I am sure that I see the mysterious woman peeking through the gap in the trees. There is a single light post on this side of the complex; it gives just enough light to see the woman's shape in the trees. I curl up on the foot of my bed and rest my chin on the cold windowsill. If it's cold in here, it must be freezing out there. The woman is there. I can see her. She's staying in the tree branches this time. I can see why—the guard is marching back and forth along the complex wall. He is looking straight ahead, so he hasn't seen the woman in the trees. She waves at me! I hesitantly wave back. She uses her fingers to make weird gestures at me again. I wish I knew what she was trying to say.

I shake my head and shrug my shoulders. The guard stops and walks up to my window. I can't see his face through his helmet, but I know he is looking right at me. He then turns to see who or what I have been gesturing at. The woman is gone. Thank goodness. I smile sheepishly at the guard and shut the blind. I climb into bed and try not to feel unsettled as I fall asleep.

Chapter 8

MORNING VICTUALS SMELL SO GOOD as our trays are brought in. Bacon! Avra is chipper and happier this morning than she was last night. Everyone else apparently smelled the bacon as the trays were brought in by the cooks, too. The tables are completely full except for three spots with the sick red-button girls again. Avra and I sit down and start digging into our bacon and eggs. I can't believe how hungry I am.

A red-button girl sitting across from me finishes her victuals and makes a low, whining sound as she uses her fingers to make weird gestures. Mentor Roberta walks to our table and starts gesturing with her fingers too. Huh...

I can't hold back my curiosity. "Mentor Roberta, what are you doing?"

She frowns at me as she answers, "Dahlia can't hear, so she communicates with her hands. It's called sign language."

Aha! I knew the mysterious woman was trying to communicate with me with her hands. "Why haven't we all learned it then? We should all be able to communicate with her."

Mentor Roberta huffs, "Dahlia is rather sickly. She doesn't leave her bedroom that much, and she will start a job in the laundry soon since schooling isn't doing her much good. It is too much work to teach you all when you will rarely see her to use it."

I try not to let Mentor Roberta see how angry her insensitivity makes me. Poor Dahlia. "Can Avra and I learn it at least? I think Dahlia deserves to have more friends to communicate with than just mentors."

Mentor Roberta huffs and looks at her clipboard. "I would normally say that your regular studies keep you too busy to add anything else. But, your grades are exceptional, Elira. So, um, okay. If you insist. I'll ask Mentor Bridget to teach you two during exploration time, but you must assure me that Avra won't fall behind."

Avra frowns and jabs me in the side with her elbow.

I smile sweetly at them both. "I'll help Avra keep up with her studies. Thank you, Mentor Roberta."

DURING SCHOOL TIME, I swipe an extra piece of paper from Mentor Bridget's desk. Andric would be so proud of me. I write down everything that I learned from Mentor Maxine last night. Avra is bouncing with anticipation because she gets the first turn on the phone today. As soon as exploration time starts, I run to the glass and press my paper up to it. Rocky, Garth, Jefrey, Bicep, and Bryon rush to the glass to read what I've written. They all nod. They seem to have suspected what I found out. I write a new question on the back of my paper. *Did you guys have white frosted cookies for victuals yesterday or today?*

The boys all shake their heads. Hmm.

Rocky presses a message to the glass, *We only get desserts like that on special occasions.*

I write back, *Yeah. Us too.*

Rocky looks at me like he's trying to decide if I can handle what he has to say. He writes, *What is your earliest memory? Do you remember life before the complex?*

Wow, this guy doesn't mess around with small talk, does he? I will have to think about that.

"Elira, it's your turn to use the phone!" Avra calls out to

me as the timer goes off. Oh, I forgot that I was right after Avra on the sign-up sheet. I walk to the white, corded telephone and take it from Avra. A handsome face with a yellow button greets me on the other side of the glass. My cheeks burn as Jefrey places the phone next to his ear.

"H-Hello?" I say in a choked voice.

A deep, smooth voice answers back, "Hello, Elira."

I feel my hands start to sweat and shake. That voice is different than any voice I've ever heard before. It's so... appealing. I think he can tell how unnerved I am because his eyes light up and they don't leave my face for even a second.

"I'm sorry, I-I have never heard such a deep voice before. It's amazing to my ears."

Jefrey smiles at me and laughs. I could listen to that happy sound all day. His blue jumpsuit is unzipped a little bit at the top. I can see that he has a purplish birthmark, or scar, very similar to mine on his left collarbone. I point at my own collarbone, temporarily forgetting that I can use my voice to communicate with him. "Is that your deformity? It's the same color as mine."

"Oh, yeah. I have several big splotches of purple. My clothes cover them up pretty well."

"That's lucky. My clothes don't cover mine, obviously."

Jefrey's blue eyes flick toward my raccoon eye. "I like your half-raccoon mask. It makes you look mysterious."

My stomach flips when his deep voice says that. "Oh, well,

thank you. I assumed that everyone thought I was ugly. I get called raccoon face a lot."

"You're the furthest thing from ugly that I've ever seen. Don't listen to them."

My mouth feels dry, "I—I won't. What is your brother's deformity?"

Jefrey gives Garth a dismissive look. "His pinky finger and his ring finger are stuck together on his right hand. So are the other two fingers on that same hand. Haven't you noticed?" The other four boys crowd in closer to try to hear my response.

I look at Garth's hands and am surprised to see that it's true. "No, I haven't noticed, till you said something."

Jefrey punches Garth in the shoulder playfully. "My brother is a three-fingered weirdo." Garth is watching me with his clear blue eyes. He puts his right hand behind his back when he sees me looking at it. I don't know why he is so self-conscious. With eyes like his, who would waste time looking at his hands?

"Where is Rocky's button? I can see that one of his ears is gone."

Jefrey rolls his eyes and looks at Rocky as he says, "Rocky is going to be charged as a dissident if he isn't careful. He can't hear out of that ear or hole, I guess. He is supposed to be wearing an orange button. He doesn't wear it like he should because he says that it isn't anyone's business to know what is wrong with him."

63

I think about that for a second. "Huh, I have never thought about it, but he has a point…"

The smile on Jefrey's face disappears. "Dissidents go away and don't come back, Elira. Rocky and Andric should follow the rules."

I laugh humorlessly. "I've seen Andric taking things apart in your school room."

Jefrey turns to look at Bicep as he answers, "Exactly, if you've seen him do it, just imagine who else has seen him, too." Bicep rolls his eyes.

Vanessa, my roommate who's afraid of windows, grabs the telephone out of my hand. "Your turn is up. It's my turn now." Of course it is.

Jefrey's eyes droop. He drops the telephone from his ear right before another boy rips it out of his hand like a hotcake. He holds up a hand to say goodbye. My heart skips a beat. The other boys hold up their hands too. I self-consciously grin and raise my hand also.

I feel a tap on my shoulder. I turn around to see Mentor Bridget standing there with her arms crossed over her chest. "Elira, I was told I need to give you sign language lessons during exploration time. We only have ten minutes left, let's get started."

I shrug and wave at the five smart boys, then join Avra and Mentor Bridget at her desk. She hands me a book with pictures of hands in weird positions. She flips to the beginning of chapter two. "This is the sign language alphabet. Every letter of our alphabet has its own sign. She shows me her closed fist with her thumb on the outside. This is an A. I want you to be able to do the entire alphabet without help then I'll teach you some simple signs for words. You can practice during your exploration time."

This is exactly what I need. "Okay. I can't wait to learn this. Thanks, Mentor Bridget."

"You're welcome. I need a drink; I'll be right back."

Avra rolls her eyes at me. "Why did you insist that we learn this? I don't want to communicate with Dahlia that much. I need my free time." She makes a pouty face as she waves at Scott on the other side of the glass. I turn to watch Scott wave back at her. I also notice Andric sliding a box of chemistry stirring rods up his sleeve.

"It's not Dahlia that I want to communicate with…"

Chapter 9

AHH! THE GUARD PLANTS HIMSELF right in front of my window now that it's bedtime. What a jerk. I really look forward to this secret bedtime ritual. I haven't even told Avra that I want to communicate with the mysterious woman yet. This is my thing. I grumpily get myself ready for bed. Vanessa clears her throat behind me. Great, the annoyance continues.

"The other girls and I have had a little discussion about you."

Please don't say anything about my stupid window. "Yeah, that's nice," I say unenthusiastically as I pin a yellow button on the gray jumpsuit I plan to wear tomorrow.

Vanessa plants her feet near the head of my bed and folds her arms in front of her. She probably thinks that she looks intimidating. "We have decided that it isn't fair that you have five boys when there aren't enough boys for all of us to have one."

I can't believe what I'm hearing. Everyone around here needs to get a life. "Uh, I don't have any boys."

Vanessa stomps her foot. "Whatever, you had five boys crowded around the telephone with you today."

I hold my hands up in surrender. "If they choose to communicate with me, that's their choice. They are interested in intellectual stuff like I am." Vanessa does not look satisfied. "If you want to win one of them over, start doing the extra credit problems."

Vanessa scoffs at me. "What's the point of doing extra credit problems? We're all going to end up at a job in a year or two no matter what our school grades are."

"Maybe that is the point. Only certain kinds of people want to challenge their minds, and those kinds of people want to hang out together."

"You are the most aggravating person I have ever met!" Vanessa says as she stomps her foot and storms off.

I turn my head to see Mentor Maxine watching me by the door. Oh, boy. She probably didn't like that. I shrug my shoulders and plop down on my bed. Mentor Maxine walks over and sits next to me on my bed. "You do seem to have more male friends than female friends, Elira."

I pull my hair back and start braiding it. "I try to be nice to everyone. I just don't have much patience for drama or fluff."

Mentor Maxine's eyes follow my birthmark from my eye to my ear. "Do you feel like you aren't challenged enough here? Do you ever wish for more?"

Longing bursts from my chest. "Yes. I do. Is there any way to see more, or do more, here at the complex?"

Mentor Maxine purses her lips together and doesn't answer for a long time. "I wish there was."

I sigh in frustration. "I've never felt confined here before, but lately, I want more knowledge, more space, and more freedom."

Mentor Maxine pats my knee. "I think you are doing all that you can do for now. When you have a job, you can see more of the complex, and you can challenge yourself in whatever field you end up in. I still think you'd make an excellent chemist. You could even be a guard. They have the most outside freedom of any job."

Yeah, but that doesn't help my frustration now, does it? I think of Rocky's questions, and decide which one to ask her. "How long have I been here, Mentor Maxine? I can't remember life before the complex."

Mentor Maxine pats my hand. "You were too young to

remember your life before this. Everyone who gets a place at the complex is placed when they are two years old."

I already knew that. "I know it costs a lot of money to get a place here. Do you think my parents loved me more than they loved themselves?"

Mentor Maxine smiles and nods. "Yes, I'm sure they did."

"Do you think they might still be alive?"

Mentor Maxine tilts her head to the side and looks at me before answering. "I'm not supposed to talk about things that aren't necessary for you to know. But since you're the only one who ever asks me anything interesting, I'll indulge you a little bit." That brings a smile to my face. Maxine looks at her boring black shoes as she answers, "There is a chance that they are still alive."

That little tidbit of hope makes me so happy. "Do you think that they live in a complex of apartment like you do?"

Mentor Maxine chokes on her own spit. "Uh, well, yes. It is likely that they would live in something like that."

I look out my window. "I'm truly grateful that my parents wanted to save me, but I wonder if I'm missing something by not growing up out there, with them."

Mentor Maxine bites her lip and nods in a barely perceptible way.

"I remember that time you held me after Heidi died. I felt... warm inside. I think that's what my parents would have done if we had lived together. You are the only mentor here who even cares about me." I look from her face to the floor. "I don't know why that matters to me all of the sudden, but it does."

It almost looks like Mentor Maxine wipes a tear from her eye. "I don't know about that, Elira. The night time mentors, Sally and Charlene, have told me that they care about you."

I balk at that thought. "They always start their shifts after we're in bed and leave as we start schooling. We hardly ever get to see them. If they cared, they would try to talk to us more."

"They are shy. They told me that they like the night shift because they don't want to talk to you girls if they have a choice."

I slap my hand on my leg. "See, they don't care about us then."

"No, for some personalities, it's hard to have to speak... about certain things. You teenagers can be an intimidating lot, even for me."

"I have to be honest, Mentor Maxine. Since we moved to the glass dorm, for the first time in my life, I want to go outside. I would really like to go out there and see the world for myself." I look hopefully into Mentor Maxine's eyes. "I could wear a guard suit."

Mentor Maxine shakes her head. "That is an impossibility unless you become a guard. Take advantage of what you have here in the complex to find answers, Elira. I have to go check on the sick reds, good night." Mentor Maxine gets up and leaves the room.

Why does she always leave when the conversation is getting good? It's so irritating. Almost as maddening as the guard standing in front of my window. I trudge into the bathroom to brush my teeth. I smile half-heartedly at the three girls with tiny heads washing their faces. I am still stirred up inside as I climb into bed. As I pull the covers up to my chin, I see the guard walk away from my window. My ears reach out to the room around me. All I hear are snores and heavy breathing. I think I'm the only one still awake in the room. I quietly slip out of my covers and stand next to the window.

The guard has his back to me and is walking away. I look at the gap in the trees. The one outside light on this side of the building is placed perfectly to shine on that spot. The woman is there looking at me. I hesitantly wave at her. She waves back. She picks up a rock and extends it toward me. She starts shaking it at me. I don't have a clue what that is supposed to mean. I use my right hand to sign A, B, C, D, the only letters I was able to master today. She nods her head and starts clapping. She puts the rock down, pushes her curly hair behind her ears, and signs five different things at me. I know that the third one is a C. I don't know any of the other ones though. The guard turns around and starts walking toward my window. The woman disappears, and I climb back into bed. I know what I will work on tomorrow.

Chapter 10

I WAIT FOR MENTOR BRIDGET to ask the question I know she will. Everyone seems to be staring off into space, ignoring what she's saying. Oh, here it comes.

"We have ten minutes left till exploration time. Do you have any questions?"

My hand shoots up into the air, because all I have in my brain right now is questions. Everyone around me rolls their eyes. They want a few extra minutes of exploration time. Mentor Bridget is surprised. "Yes, Elira?"

"I would like to learn about the history of the world. When did the pollution start, and when did the chemical warfare end?"

The glaze covering everyone's eyes disappears, and the girls around me sit up taller. We all look at Mentor Bridget expectantly. She is shuffling papers on her desk, not looking at us. I think she's preparing her response. She looks up. "That is a long, boring story that I don't think would benefit you much. Your lives are preserved and protected inside the complex, and knowing the misfortune of those on the outside will not make your lives as future complex workers any better."

Mara, the boss of the world, raises her hand, "I think I will work harder knowing that I'm keeping the few remaining survivors of the world fed, clothed, and happy."

Mentor Bridget smiles and nods. "And so you shall. That's all that needs to be said about it. It's exploration time now; use your time wisely." Girls stand up and move to their friends' desks or the glass wall. Their momentary curiosity is gone.

I stay in my desk, drowning in disappointment. That was the most unhelpful response I could have received. Even Mentor Roberta has given me more information about the outside than that. Mentor Bridget opens her sign language book as she walks toward me and sets it on my desk. I think it's her nonverbal way of saying I better move on to other things now. Fine. I'll work on my sign language. As soon as I am fluent in it, the woman on the outside will give me answers. I just know it.

The scratch paper I'm using, left over from math, is almost full of my sign language notes. I wish I could walk up to Mentor Bridget's desk and take a stack of papers for my own use, but we aren't allowed more paper than our assignments require. I also wish I was a better artist. I try my best to copy the letters and hand shapes from the book, but I have to hurry, and my hand shapes look like a five-year-old drew them. At my current rate, I will only get through the letter J.

Avra is still mad at me about these extra lessons. She grumbles at me as she draws little hand shapes, "You have no right to take all my exploration time for this stupid stuff, Elira."

I lean closer to Avra and whisper, "If we know how to sign things with our hands, then we can communicate with the boys through the glass better, you know."

Avra's droopy posture perks up. "Huh, I hadn't thought of that." She looks at the girls pressing their homework papers to the glass, and nods. "I will tell Scott that he should learn too."

I turn around and see my five boys looking at me through the glass with curiosity and impatience. I wish I had more time, so I could tell them what I'm doing. Surely, they can kind of figure it out.

I wonder if I can slip back in here after 5:00 victuals and see if any boys at all are in their school room. They could go get someone from my smart gang—I have decided to call Jefrey, Garth, Rocky, Andric, and Bryon my smart gang. When Mentor Bridget leaves to use the bathroom, I sneak a piece of paper and a pencil to tell the boys what I am doing during exploration time. When she returns, and the loud shriek noise goes off. I wave at my gang and point at my folded paper. Andric nods at me as he takes a box of matches off an experiment station and slips it down the neck of his jumpsuit. Matches, Bicep, what are you going to do with those? I can't get the image of him doing that out of my head as I hurry out of the room to eat.

The chicken noodle soup we get for 5:00 victuals is incredibly good. I feel funny eating it with the squarish spoon they gave me though. I thought all spoons were oval before moving into this dorm. Avra thinks they give us fancier utensils in the glass dorm, so we will feel grown up, ready to take on jobs soon.

Sniff, sniff. Is someone sniffing me?

"Not only do you look funny and ask funny questions, you smell funny too," Julie says as she shakes her dark-brown hair out of her face. Oh great. I've been trying to avoid this girl.

She's just getting started. "I've been filling out my job interest paper today. I wonder what job you'll get stuck with. No one will want to see you or smell you, so I'm betting you'll get to be a janitor or a laundry worker."

I do a quick armpit sniff and feel like I pass. My hand tightens around my spoon. I don't know why she hates me, but this is ridiculous. I have done nothing to her, yet... "Well, we members of the yellow club have to do our part, don't we?" I say as I dump my glass of water down her neck. Julie shrieks, frozen in place with shock.

"Oops, sorry!" I say sarcastically as I turn around and jet out of the room. I still have the weird spoon in my hand as I leave the rest of my victuals and run to my room. I'm glad I have my paper and pencil in my pocket. I shut the door to my room and push the closest bed in front of it, so no one can get in. *Thud, wham, bam.* I hear Julie trying to push her way in. I shove all my weight against the bed and door. There is no way I'm letting her in.

"I won't forget this, Elira!" She yells through the door. She smacks the door loudly one last time and then walks away.

I'm sure she won't forget, but I don't care. I have more important things to worry about. My spoon trades spots with the paper and pencil in my pocket. I kneel down beside the bed I moved, I think it's Shasta's, and write down everything I have seen out my window and every conversation I've had with Mentor Maxine. The thought of pressing it up to the glass for every boy to see makes me squirm. I wish there was a way to get more privacy in the school room.

I move the bed away from the door. I'm sure someone will want in here soon. I walk to the window and plop down on my bed with the folded letter in my hand. I take some deep breaths and tell myself that the boys are probably more paranoid than they should be about this place. They haven't even punished me for my outburst.

"Ahem." Mentor Roberta clears her throat as she walks into my room. I guess I spoke too soon.

I quickly shove the folded letter into my pocket and sit up. "I'm sorry. I lost my temper."

Mentor Roberta looks at me silently for a minute. "I am trying to decide if this is a one-time event, or if you need to start certain... medication to keep your emotions in check."

I sit up and look at Mentor Roberta's hairy chin. "Julie said unkind things to me, Mentor... but I shouldn't have reacted. It was a one-time event. I promise it won't happen again."

"It better not, or you will spend an eight-hour shift in the dirtiest corner of the laundry room."

I stop mid-complaint and think about that threat. I actually might like that. It would be a chance to leave my dorm for once and maybe even learn some of the complex's secrets. "I am in control of myself, I promise."

Mentor Roberta and her clipboard exit the room. Avra walks in with a big frown on her face. "What is wrong with you? You know what Julie is like. If you can't keep it together, you'll get charged as a dissident."

Dissident, what a funny word. Dissidents are people who cause trouble in the complex. I knew one who was always starting fights and breaking things, I knew another who was always trying to escape our dorm. I wonder if she was trying to go outside like I kind of want to. They were taken from our dorm and they never came back. I wonder what really happened to them. "Avra, how many dissidents have we known?"

Avra pauses to think. "I can only remember one, years ago. She was sent out of the complex to live in the toxic world."

"Hmm. I can remember two. Why are there so few? Don't people ever want to tear this structured world apart? I know I do."

"Elira, don't. Don't ask why. Instead, let's ask how. How can we see the boys one more time tonight?"

I laugh to myself. "I can't believe I like you so much when you are this shallow. But, now that you mention it, I bet if we volunteer to clean the school room, we could get an extra hour next to the glass wall."

"Let's try!"

"Okay."

We look for Mentor Roberta and find her in the bathroom vanity area with a sick red. I make my face look as remorseful as I can. "Mentor Roberta, I feel terrible about losing my temper. Can I make it up to you by cleaning the desks and the whiteboards in the school room? I know I would feel better."

Mentor Roberta looks at me sideways for a moment and then looks down at her clipboard. "Yes, Elira. That would help make up for your outburst."

"May Avra come too?"

She looks at Avra, then back at me. Does she suspect something? "Yes, if her heart is up to it."

"Oh, I'm pretty sure her heart is up to it."

We turn and leave. As soon as we're out of eyesight,

we laugh and run to the school room. There are five girls in there, already flirting with boys through the glass. They have cleaning rags in their hands; they must have made the same kind of excuses to be here. Avra and I talk to Liza who is on the telephone again. We ask if someone can get our boys to come to the glass. They say they will get them for us.

Avra and I clean the whiteboards and desks like mad-women. When we're done, we see Scott and Garth waiting for us at the glass. Avra runs up to the glass as giggly as Liza. I wish I could hide my raccoon eye as Garth's intense stare penetrates me. He seems happy to see me. I wobble as I slowly approach the window. It's like his blue eyes can see through the tough face that I force myself to wear, to the worried, insecure girl underneath. I swear I can sense his warmth through the glass. I wish I could touch him. I put my hand on the glass, but the barrier between us is as cold and hard as ice. I slowly pull the letter I have written out of my pocket and press it to the glass. Scott breaks eye contact with Avra and tries to read my paper. Garth immediately shakes his head and gestures for me to take the paper down.

Great, now what do I do? Garth points at the left end of the glass wall. I walk clear to the end of the glass. This should give us some privacy. Actually, now that I'm looking, there is a metal grate on the wall that pulls air out of the room. I wonder if I can stick the letter in there.

I move down the glass wall to see what is on the boys' side

of the wall. It looks like they have a grate in the same spot. Ha! How have I not noticed that? I squat down and say into the grate, "Garth, can you hear me?"

Nothing, silence. The complex staff must have known we'd figure out how to speak into it. There is some kind of sound barrier in there.

Ow, something in my pocket is poking me as I squat. Ooh! I have an idea. I take the squarish spoon out of my pocket and see if it will fit into the screw heads. It does! The spoon makes a clumsy screwdriver, but I slowly get a screw out. Garth nods and smiles down at me through the glass.

Avra looks over at me and comes unglued. "What are you doing, Elira?"

"I'm making a way to pass notes to the boys. Stand guard at the door for me, please?"

Avra looks furtively at the other girls in the room. They are oblivious to what we're doing. They are crowded around the telephone with boys on the other side who are doing the same thing. "Okay, Elira. You owe me, and you only get five minutes." She blows a kiss to Scott and then marches to the door.

I work as quickly as my hands can. I get another screw out. Garth is trying to block what I'm doing from Scott on the other side while he talks to him. I get three more screws out and notice that the metal face plate is loose and will swivel up and over with only one screw left in the wall. Woohoo! Garth gives me a wink and a thumbs-up while he pretends to stretch. It doesn't work. Scott can totally tell what I'm doing. Luckily, he'll benefit from this too. I get on my hands and knees and stick my head into the 12-inch square hole that is now exposed in the wall. *Bonk*. My forehead hits something I can't see. Cold air tugs my hair down. There is a clear sound barricade inside the cold air return. I must not be the first person to try to speak through it. I wiggle the square piece of plexiglass and pull it out of the hole. I can see the slotted metal plate on the boys' side of the wall less than a foot away. Do I dare speak through it?

I tap the metal softly with my fingers first, "Garth?"

He taps back, "Elira?"

I try not to tremble as I hear that deep, alluring voice, so similar to his brother's. "I don't have much time, Garth, but we should try to do this again soon. Take this letter. I have written down everything I know about odd things at the complex." I shove the folded paper through one of the metal slots on his side.

"Thank you. Rocky will be thrilled, but be careful, Elira."

"Why?"

"Have you noticed anything different about my group of friends?"

I smile as I think about how good looking they are. I'm not going to say that though. "You guys are the smart ones."

Garth laughs. "Well, thanks, we like to think so, but have you noticed anything else?"

"Andric takes things apart and steals things."

"Yeah, that makes him stand out, doesn't it? He is trying to find a way out of here. I can't believe he didn't figure out how to take this cold air return apart already. Oh, it looks like he tried, but he destroyed the screw heads. Ha! He can't stand sitting around being told what to do 24/7."

"I hope the mentors haven't noticed the same things I have. They will charge him as a dissident."

"Yeah, that's the problem. They have noticed. He is being watched, and we are his friends, so we are being watched too. I'm afraid you'll be watched on your side for your interest in us."

"Elira! Could you bring me another cleaning rag, please?"

I take that as a sign from Avra. "I have to go. Bye, Garth."

"Bye, Elira."

Oh! That's my name coming out of his lips. *Tremble, tremble.* My hands don't want to work as I force the soundproof plexiglass back in place and then slide the square metal cover back into its worn grooves. I stand up just as Mentor Roberta walks into the room. Garth quickly leaves his school room before he is recognized. I hide the loose screws in my left fist as I walk across the room with a smile on my face and a rag in my right hand. "Here you are, Avra. I think we're about done. We should go to bed. I'm tired."

"Yeah... me too." Avra hesitantly agrees as she looks at Scott's disappointed face.

Mentor Roberta frowns as she watches us put our cleaning

supplies away. We smile at her and leave the room. My heart is beating a thousand times a minute as I walk down the hall. My hands are shaking. I just hope that Mentor Roberta's attention is drawn to our retreating backs and not to the unscrewed grate cover in the back corner of the school room.

Chapter 11

THE GUARD IS STANDING IN FRONT of my window again tonight. Blast him! I wonder if I really am being watched... To be honest with myself, I don't know what the mysterious woman is signing yet. I know there is a C, and I'm pretty sure there is a K as well. I'll know tomorrow when I finish my sign language alphabet. Avra rolls over in bed and whispers to me, "Did you get your letter through the grate?"

I can't hide the smile on my face. "Yep!"

Avra grins from ear to ear as she stares at the ceiling. "I'm going to write Scott a letter tomorrow. Will you stick it through the grate for me?"

I can't help but giggle. "Yes. Thank you for standing guard tonight."

"You're welcome. Did you see Mentor Roberta's face when she came in? It was almost like she was sure she'd find us breaking the rules."

I look at her incredulously. "We were breaking the rules."

"I know. We need to be careful, but man, am I excited about this new letter hole!"

I don't let Avra know that as excited as I am, I'm also equally scared that they'll discover what I've done and charge me as a dissident. "Yeah, Avra. Me too."

"Which of your boy gang do you like the most?"

I pause and think about my smart gang before answering. "They are all handsome in their own way, but two of them are tied in my mind. Who do you think I like the most?"

"Well, when one of the twins looks at you, I swear you stop breathing."

I blush under the edge of my blanket. "Yeah, I like the twins. My eyes find them no matter how crowded their school room is." Avra giggles.

Words keep spilling out of my mouth without my permission, "Oh, and their voices... Their voices sound as nice as butter tastes on hot bread." Avra smiles as she reaches out and nudges my arm. I take a deep breath and let it out to slow down my heart. "I'm not sure which one I like the most, Avra. They both make me weak in the knees."

Avra rolls onto her side to look at me better. "Which one do you have the most in common with?"

"I don't know. I've only spoken to each of them once."

"Good point. Can you even tell them apart? I can't."

I giggle in exasperation. "As far as looks go, not really. Jefrey has a yellow button and some purple marks like mine. Garth's fingers are stuck together on one hand and has an orange button. That's literally the only way I can tell them apart without speaking to them."

"Ha ha! Good luck with that!"

"Yeah." I sigh. I like them both. The same. So far.

MENTOR BRIDGET CLAPS HER HANDS with delight. "Welcome to job research weeks everyone!" The older girls smile and cheer while we 16 girls just stare blankly at her. "Each day for the next 12 days, we will have professional workers from the 12 jobs come into the school room to help teach skills used in their particular job. Today is cooking day." Avra claps her hands happily. I guess this means I won't be working on my sign language for a while. Dang. Oh well, the guard keeps standing in front of my window anyway.

Six cooks enter the school room dressed in purple jumpsuits. They bring in rolling carts filled with fruits, vegetables, dry powders, slimy pink stuff, and many other weird looking things that I can't name. We all gape as they set up machines and ingredients at six of the experiment stations around the room.

Mentor Bridget clears her throat. "There are six stations that you will rotate through. At each one you will make something different. There is a green salad station, a fruit salad station, a waffle station, a meat station, a soup station, and a pudding station. You will be making your own noon and 5:00 victuals. These cooks usually make them for you, but they are in here today. So, it is in your best interest not to mess anything up too badly. Get in groups of 10 and get to work!"

I just love how everyone is in a group before I've even had time to process what is happening. Avra tugs on my sleeve. "There's only room left at the meat station, let's go!"

"Okay, okay." I look at the meat station with its cutting boards and electric things I've never seen before plugged into the wall, and then I look at the girls in that group. Oh goody. We're with Mara and Julie. Gee, I wonder why no one else wants to be in this group. "At least we aren't with Vanessa..." I mutter under my breath as I pull a black apron over my head.

"Look who came to join us, Mara," Julie says as she slides a blob of pink slimy stuff on a cutting board toward me. "It's raccoon face and baldy."

I turn from Julie's smug face to our cook's sweet, light-brown face. "I'm sorry, but I don't know if it will be safe to have these two and me in the same area with knives."

The cook's smile slides right off her face. "Really, girls? I wanted this to be a fun day. Fine. I'll go get Mentor Bridget to babysit you three."

Oh no. That's not what I want. "Why can't I switch groups?"

The usually smiley cook points around the room. "Everyone in the other groups has already started their recipes. You'll just have to learn to get along. Now wash your hands and start chopping your chicken into bite-sized pieces while I get Mentor Bridget."

We wash our hands obediently at the experiment station sink. Julie watches the cook talk to Mentor Bridget, turns to her cutting board, and starts chopping her pink glob with more force than is necessary. "I would back up if I were you, Elira."

"I think I will. Thanks for the suggestion," I say sarcastically as I scoot as far away from Julie as possible. Avra scoots next to me. "When is she going to give us the chicken, Avra?"

"I think this pink stuff is the chicken."

"Uh, I've eaten a lot of chicken in my life. It's not pink and slimy. It's white, and sometimes it's browned a bit."

"We haven't cooked it yet. It will probably turn white."

"Oh, right."

The cook finds her smile again once Mentor Bridget is planted behind me. "I am going to get the frying pans and woks heating up, so don't touch them, or you'll get burned." I scoot a few inches away from the nearest pan.

As hard as it is to have Julie, Mara, and Mentor Bridget glaring at me as I chop, it's kind of fun to watch Avra thriving in this environment. She was right, the pink slimy chicken did turn white when we put it in the hot frying pans and electric woks provided.

"Elira, you cook your chicken chunks with that olive oil stuff and that bottle of seasonings, and I'll cook mine without anything. Let's see which tastes better."

"Okay, you're on."

I turn around to see if the boys are doing this same thing today. They are. Bicep is at the chicken cutting station too and I see him stick a knife up his sleeve. It makes my heart race just imagining a loose knife flopping around in my sleeve. Oh, he just asked to go to the bathroom. He's good at what he does, I admit. "Ow!" My skin screams at me as I shove the back of my hand in my mouth. The olive oil pops and snaps out of the pan when it's hot. When I've calmed myself down, I take my hand out of my mouth and watch a red spot appear before my eyes.

"Hey, Mara. Raccoon face is adding more splotches to her body. Do you think she knows that the rest of us aren't following her fashion trend?" Mara laughs out loud until Mentor Bridget makes her stop.

"You're right, Julie. Maybe I should be rude and nasty to everyone I meet so I can be fashionable like you."

"Enough, you two," Mentor Bridget says, "One more outburst and I'll send you both to a solitary cell. This is supposed to be fun and educational. Stop ruining it for everyone around you." Julie turns her back to me, which suits me just fine. I only open my mouth if she does.

Avra and I do a taste test on our chicken once it's done. Mine is a little bit darker than it probably should be. I've been a little bit distracted in this hostile environment. Avra's chicken is the perfect golden-brown color. I try a bite from both pans. "Avra, I think yours is cooked to the perfect doneness, but I think the oil and seasonings on mine give it better flavor."

Avra tries some chicken from both pans and nods in agreement. "You're right. I will cook my next batch with oil and seasonings."

Her next batch is perfectly delicious—even our smiley cook wants to try it. Avra knows what her gift is, and I'm kind of jealous. I don't care that I'm not a natural at cooking, but I wish I knew what job I am meant for.

Mentor Bridget looks at the clock. She announces to the room at large, "You have fifteen minutes to clean up then switch to the station on your left."

The chicken residue in my pan takes more scrubbing than I expect it to. I get it clean just in time for the next group to kick me out of my spot.

We switch stations. We make green salad. We switch again. Avra impresses each cook we work with. I barely keep from getting in a fight with Julie each time Mentor Bridget turns her back. What a day.

The victuals are delicious at least. We have chicken on green salad with pudding for noon victuals and chicken noodle soup with fruit salad for 5:00 victuals. The other half of the room does the opposite. The waffles are eaten as soon as they come off the waffle irons as what Mentor Bridget calls 'a snack.' I think it means eating something during unappointed times. The waffles are our last station, and Avra needs a chair to sit on through the whole thing. She stirs the batter while I run the waffle iron. I get nervous when Mentor Bridget writes something on her clipboard. *Please don't take this away from her,* I beg Mentor Bridget in my head. *Please don't take away the one job she loves. She is meant to cook.*

Mentor Bridget clears her throat loudly. "Girls, may I have your attention? You did a wonderful job today, some more than others. That is the way it is supposed to be. As the job research days go on, you will notice what comes naturally to you and what does not. You'll then be able to make an informed choice when filling out your job interest papers. Get a good night's rest, and we'll see you all back here tomorrow for gardening day."

We are all surprisingly tired after we clean up the school room and send the cooks away with their wheeled carts. Hardly anyone even tries to flirt with the boys before we're kicked out of the room. Is this what having a job feels like? Twelve days of this in a row seems like a lot. I guess I better get used to it. When I turn 18, I'll have the same job the rest of my days in a row.

Chapter 12

GARDENING DAY IS FUN. The gardeners wheel in carts full of bagged soil, seeds, and tiny pots. I like planting seeds in little-tiny pots. We are told that the tomato and cucumber plants we plant today will be planted in the outside soil once they get too big for their pots. I start to think I should be a gardener if it means I can wander around outside.

Mentor Bridget overhears my group talking and clarifies something. "For those of you who don't know, the complex is a giant octagon with a basement, a main floor and a second floor. The dorms are mostly on the second floor, you have probably guessed this because there are occasionally windows in the dorms. You probably remember being moved down a flight of stairs once you were moved to the wooden dorm. That dorm and the glass dorm are the only ones on the main floor. Half of the jobs in the complex are located in the basement, like cooking, laundry, textiles, and chemistry. The other half are on the main floor, like artistry, metal welding, and gardening. The gardens are located in the center of the octagon with a glass ceiling to let the sun in. So, gardeners can't wander off into the toxic world, and no outsiders can steal our vegetables."

Well, never mind. I don't want to be a gardener then.

THE NEXT DAY IS JANITORIAL DAY. I am dead set against doing this job after scrubbing the left-side bathroom from top to bottom with only a tiny brush to separate my hand from the grime. But then one of the janitors tells me something that changes my mind.

"When I chuck bags of garbage out the garbage chute, I see daylight through the flaps. It's my favorite part of the day. It's beautiful." That's pretty cool.

I turn to Avra, who's scrubbing the base of a toilet. "If I was a janitor, I could stick my arm out the garbage chute and feel the sun and the wind that I'm so curious about."

The janitor who is helping us notices my excitement and clarifies, "No, missy. We wear protective suits when we send things out the garbage chute. You can't feel a thing. We don't want to absorb toxins doing that."

"Oh." Never mind.

TEXTILE DAY IS TERRIBLE. My back is absolutely killing me. I glare at pillowcase number 12 as I feed it through my sewing machine. How many pillowcases can this complex possibly need anyway? The boys sew pillowcases all day too. I can tell Andric is frustrated with his sewing machine. He's trying to do a two-handed job with his one good arm. I watch as he pounds the table he's working at in frustration and the sewing machine falls off the table onto the floor. Parts and pieces go flying, and Andric is escorted from the room by a tall, chocolatey-brown mentor with biceps almost as big as his own. I catch Garth's eye after Andric is gone. I wish I could communicate with him. I need to meet with him, but there are too many mentors and workers on both sides of the glass during job research weeks.

ON GUARD DAY I AM HOPEFUL that we'll get to leave the complex. Ha ha ha. Nope. Four guards come into our school room wearing their white protective suits. I can't tell them apart other than they stand at different heights. When they push a button at neck level, the helmet detaches from the rest of the suit. All four helmets come off at the same time. I am surprised to see a woman and three men staring back at me. I am paying attention today. This may be the job for me.

The woman does most of the talking once the helmets come off. "Who would like to try on a protective guard suit?" About half of the girls in the room raise their hands. I am one of them. Avra is not. I am shocked at how heavy and claustrophobic the suit makes me feel once the helmet is latched on. Ahh, I feel like I can't breathe. When I touch the guard next to me, it doesn't register in my brain that I am touching skin. I feel like a plastic person touching plastic things. Ahh! Get me out of here! I press the button on my neck and finally breathe easy again when the helmet releases. I don't know if I want this job after all... *But I could wander around outside,* I tell myself. What good is the ability to wander around if you feel like you're going to die in an enclosed piece of plastic?

The guards set up tiny, red-colored plastic animals and people figurines around the experiment station sinks. They give each of us a plastic gun that is filled with water and tell us to shoot the plastic figurines into the sink.

Avra hates it. She misses hitting anything five times in a row. She gives up and gives me her water gun.

I tell myself that I can do this as I raise my plastic water gun. *Bam, bam, bam, miss, miss, bam.* I shoot four out of five figurines into the sink. I miss a couple more times before getting the fifth one. One of the male guards grabs my shoulder and drags me up to the front of the room. "I know you, little girl," the tall broad-shouldered man with a shaved head says as we walk.

I'm a little bit creeped out. "How can that be? I don't know you," I say as I gulp loudly.

"You like to look out the window on the south side of the complex."

I breathe a sigh of relief. This is probably the guard I've been calling a jerk every night. "Oh, yeah. My bed is right next to a window."

He breathes down my neck. "Do you look out the window because you want to be a guard like me, or do you do it so you can find ways to get in trouble?"

I answer him rapidly, "I want to be a guard. I'm a yellow, so I can. Ask Mentor Maxine, she knows I want to."

He waits a few seconds before he answers me, "I believe you, but I've been told to block your window. I'm sure it's for your own good. You're a good shot, but you'll need to overcome your fear of the suit."

I feel sweat start to form on my forehead. "Yes, sir." Great, they are watching me. I stand at the front of the room awkwardly as the winners of each experiment station are brought up next to me. I notice that all five of the boys from my smart gang are standing at the front of their room too. What do you know, we rebels know how to shoot. I am surprised and thrilled when Shasta joins me at the front of the room.

The female guard clears her throat. "We will have a shoot off amongst the six winners. They will each get an experiment station sink, five figurines, ten shots allowed. The girl who can shoot all five figurines into the sink in the least amount of shots will get an endorsement from me to become a guard. Only one girl from each age group is given a preliminary spot in the guard program. Take this seriously and aim true."

Wow. I don't feel ready for this. I wish she hadn't raised the stakes like that. I was fine when this was just for fun. I walk to the nearest experiment station, Shasta takes the next one over. I take my refilled water gun and aim it at the middle figurine. If I miss him, I have a good chance at taking out the guy next to him. *Bam.* Middle figurine down. I aim for the next figurine on the right. *Bam.* He's down too. I look at Shasta's sink, three figurines are down. Did it take her more than one shot each? I don't know. I take aim again, for the figurine to the left of the middle. *Bam.* I missed the one I was aiming for, but I hit the figurine next to him. Three down, two to go. I aim for the figurine on the left. *Miss.* Dang it, too far left. At least it's my first miss. I aim at the same one. *Bam.* Woohoo! One left to go. I aim so intently that my eyes start to cross. *Miss.* Ahh! I can do this. I aim. I wait for my eyes to see clearly again. Perfect. *Bam.* I think I did pretty well. I look around the room. Everyone is done.

"May I have your attention please? The winner of our shoot-off is the one and only... Shasta!" the female guard sings out. What? She got all five in less than seven shots?

"Getting all five figurines in five shots is an amazing feat, even for us, trained guards, so congratulations, Shasta. Unfortunately, it has come to my attention that you are a red, so you are disqualified from entering the guard program. That forces my hand in giving the coveted endorsement from me, Guard Venus, to the second-place shooter, Elira!"

I stand there stunned as a signed piece of paper is forced into my hands. Guards, mentors, and fellow dormmates congratulate me over and over again. I don't even smile at them. I am disappointed that I didn't shoot better. But I'm even more disappointed that Shasta doesn't get what she has rightfully earned and has always desired simply because she wears a red button.

Chapter 13

IT'S CHEMISTRY DAY AND I AM DETERMINED
to make contact with my gang. I have something important to
say to Shasta too. This career exploration stuff has been fun and
educational and all, but yesterday made me realize how wrong
some of the complex's ways feel to me. Even my number one
job choice feels wrong. The only people I can talk to about it are
Mentor Maxine and my smart gang.

I make sure when we're told to get into groups around
a bunsen burner, that I get into Shasta's group. Avra doesn't
follow me fast enough, and she ends up in a different group
than me for the first time this week. Oh well, we'll be fine

in different groups for a day. Shasta is avoiding my eye on purpose. I approach her several times, but she turns her body away from me. I feel terrible, but I won't be ignored. I keep walking around her until I am right in her face, or I guess, below it. "Shasta, I'm sorry about what happened during the shoot-out yesterday."

She won't look me in the eye. "Yeah, don't worry about it."

I look at my feet too. "I am, and I will worry about it. What they did was wrong and disgusting to me. Here, I want you to have this." My hand pulls a folded and crinkled piece of paper out of my pocket. I hand her the written endorsement by Guard Venus. Shasta lifts it up to her eyes, closer than I would expect. I wonder if her eyes give her problems. If they do, it makes her shooting yesterday even more impressive.

Shasta shakes her head in disbelief. "You shouldn't have crossed out your name, Elira. This paper will do me no good, but it could still do you some good."

"No. I didn't earn it. If I become a guard it will be because I earned it fair and square. I wrote your name on it because you earned it, and we all know it." I elbow Tessa who is eavesdropping next to me and she nods in agreement. I exhale, relieved that I said what I promised myself I would say. I leave Shasta to herself and start helping Tessa measure powders for our chemical compound.

The balding, male chemist helping our group sweats bullets as we measure powders. "Please don't touch any of these chemicals without gloves, girls. The green liquid in particular will burn a hole right through the table if we spill it, so be careful."

I don't need telling twice. I put on some thick rubber gloves before touching any of the liquids. When I add each ingredient, the compound changes color dramatically. It's quite thrilling! When I add the last ingredient, an interesting smell comes from our test tube.

Our chemist beams at me. "Well done! Do you know what it is?"

I shake my head as I crinkle my nose, "I have no idea."

"Toilet cleaner!" Woohoo. We're going to change the world with that. I yawn, unimpressed that my concoction is headed straight to the janitor's closet.

I look over to the glass wall just in time to see Andric winding up his enormous arm to punch the wall. *Bam, bam, bam!* I see a huge fist blast through the wall just below the enormous glass window that connects us with the boys. The fist pulls back from where it came from, then *Bam!* It bursts through the wall again. When the fist retracts this time I see Bicep's eyes peeking through the hole.

"Elira, girls, take the green fluid. It burns through things really well; finish breaking through this wall. I have a door rigged on this side that goes into the hall. It will burst into flames any second now. Get out and get out now. I've heard the mentors talking; they are going to make us their puppets. They are going to stop us from fighting back; get out now, while you…"

Two big, muscular mentors approach Andric, punching him in the face and the gut. They haul him out as he unsuccessfully fights them off. He never finishes his sentence. I hear one of them say, "This was a dumb move, dissident. You're a goner, now."

Girls around me start screaming. The chemist at our experiment station hurriedly puts all the chemicals at our table away before any of us can swipe them. I see Garth and Jefrey pushing their way toward the hole. Fear fills me as I walk closer to the hole and touch the powdery broken wall. Jefrey reaches me first, he sticks his hand through the hole and takes mine.

I yell into the hole, so I can be heard through the screaming girls, "They took him, Jefrey. They called him a dissident. He won't come back!"

Jefrey squeezes my hand. "It's okay, Elira. Don't do anything he said. You'll be okay."

Garth is pressed up against the glass now, but he can't fit his hand through the already crowded hole. I call out, "Tomorrow, nine o'clock, information, please." Garth nods and walks away. Jefrey looks at me questioningly as another mentor pulls him and the other boys away from the hole.

Mentor Bridget pushes her shriek button. We all shut up and cover our ears. "Everyone is to clear the school room. Go to your bedrooms and wait there for an hour until your 5:00

victuals arrive. No one is to enter the school room until the hole the dissident created has been patched. Do you understand?"

There are some yeses and some crying and some hysterics, but we all get the point. We need to get out of here or be charged as dissidents ourselves. Andric said my name specifically. I better get out of here and keep my nose clean all evening. I grab Avra and rush for the door. I don't stop rushing until the two of us are safely on our beds trying to slow down our breathing.

Chapter 14

I WAKE UP WITH A HEADACHE. I cried myself to sleep last night. I can't believe I will never see Andric again. I've never had a personal relationship with a dissident before. It feels awful. What is just as bad, is that I know I'm being watched too. I don't know where I am mentally, but it's not here. Avra pulls me out of the doorway as I try to zombie walk out of our room.

"Elira, you should probably brush your hair before you go eat." Oh yeah. I should do that. I see a brush sitting on Vanessa's bed and absentmindedly pick it up and start tearing through my hair. Avra doesn't say anything as she takes the brush out of my hand and puts it back on Vanessa's bed. She takes my hand and walks me to my bed. She makes me sit down and gently brushes my hair with my own brush. She then braids it into a tidy double braid. She really is the best friend a girl could have.

Mentor Roberta has an announcement for us as we congregate in the common room. She doesn't seem as affected by yesterday's happenings as we are. "Today will be your last job research day. All of the remaining jobs will be discussed by a speaker from each area, but you will not be allowed to do any more hands-on job trials."

Gee, I wonder why. The glass dorm is an absolute nightmare right now. Everyone keeps saying the most horrible things about Andric. I don't know if I can eat. My stomach is wound into a tight knot. I lay my head on the table at 7:00 victuals and hope that everyone will just shut up and leave me alone.

Avra of course doesn't leave my side. "It's not your fault. He made his own choices; now he'll have to deal with the consequences."

"What are the consequences for sure?"

Avra rubs my back gently. "I'm pretty sure they get sent into the toxic world, but some people are saying... well, who cares what they say. It will be okay, Elira."

Yeah, right. One last tear runs down my cheek, the last one left, after a night of waterworks. "There are worse things in this life than living in a toxic world, right, Avra?" I don't tell her that I fear I might be sent out there next.

Avra watches the last few girls walk to the school room door. "Yeah, I'm sure there are worse things. Don't worry about him. He wanted out. He's getting what he wanted. He's a tough guy."

Someone clears her throat behind us. "You two are going to be late. Get yourselves into the school room right now," Mentor Roberta exclaims in her usual less-than-loving way.

Avra and I avoid eye contact with her as we trudge into the school room. I stay awake through all the job lectures in the morning by sheer willpower, but I remember nothing about what is said. The hole in the wall has been patched up already. The mud isn't dry, so there are chairs and red tape blocking us from touching the area. After noon victuals I don't even pretend to listen. I lay my head down on my desk and cry myself to sleep. I keep seeing the mentors punching Andric and calling him a dissident. Am I next? What have I done?

Avra nudges me, and I jerk my head up. Drool strings from my lip to my desk. Ahh! I swipe it off with my sleeve. A few girls around me snigger as they leave the room for 5:00 victuals. I wipe my eyes and my mouth one more time, then stand up with as much dignity as I can muster and follow Avra to the dining tables. I sit down, hoping no one will talk to me.

"Hey, raccoon eye, are you sad they found out your boyfriend is a dissident?" Julie taunts with a cruel smile.

I ignore her as I pull the foil off my tray. Ooh, coconut cream pie—they must be feeling sorry for us in the kitchens. This is like a once-a-month treat. Mmm. Too bad it tastes just a tad stale.

"I'm glad you decided to go for the bad boy type. You've left the twins all to me."

What? Does she like the twins? I scowl at her. "I suggest you shut up, Julie."

"Everyone could tell that you loved Andric's big muscly arm, but only I could tell that you loved his small shriveled arm even more."

That's it. I grab my coconut cream pie and shove it in her face as I scream like a banshee.

Mentor Maxine grabs my shoulders and says as she marches me out, "You will stay in your room for the night without victuals. What an inappropriate thing to do."

As soon as we're in my room, Mentor Maxine sets me on my bed and leaves. I feel terrible. Mentor Maxine is going to hate me forever. That hurts just as much as knowing Andric is gone for good. I want to cry but the tears won't come. I curl into a ball on my bed and hope the softness of the pillow will send me to a softer place than the complex. I don't care that my hands are still sticky from the pie. I'm surprised when Mentor Maxine comes back in with a warm wet towel. She takes my pie-covered hands and washes them off. Tears stream down my cheeks. She hugs me as I let the tears fall.

"It's okay to cry, Elira. It's a terrible thing to lose a friend."

Those words take me back to when I was six. My tears fall faster. When I'm all cried out, Mentor Maxine tucks me into bed and wipes the last tear from my cheek.

I SIT UP IN BED. Everyone around me is sound asleep. I didn't even know I had fallen asleep until now. I look at the red numbers on the digital clock on the wall, 9:35. Oh no! I told Garth to meet me at 9:00. I rush out of my room and into the common room. Mentor Maxine is the only one in here. She is reading a book. "I'm sorry, Mentor Maxine. I just need to go into the school room for a few minutes, I won't be long."

Mentor Maxine looks up from her book only briefly. "Just a few minutes, then you go back to bed. You've had a couple of hard days. You need your sleep."

"Okay."

I rush into the school room and feel my heart drop as I see Garth leaving his school room. I run up to the glass and pound it as hard as I can with my fist. *Bam. Bam. Bam.*

Garth turns around at the door and sees me. He runs up to the glass and points at the grate. I rush to the metal square and swivel it up. The plexiglass barrier pops out as I give a muscly tug on it.

"Elira! I was afraid something happened to you. I didn't think you were coming."

I wipe the sleepiness out of my eyes. "I'm so sorry. I fell asleep."

"You look like you've been crying."

Great, I must look horrible. "I have. I can't believe one of my own friends is being charged as a dissident."

Garth leans his forehead against the grate. "Yeah. I know. We tried to stop him, but he was so sure that something terrible was about to happen, he wouldn't hear reason."

"Did they do anything to the rest of you?"

Garth laughs humorlessly. "It's a mentor yelling fest over here. They were not happy with us when they replaced the burned door. The other guys on this side told the mentors that Rocky, Bryon, Jefrey and I were Andric's friends, so they took us into separate rooms and questioned us all. We told them that we had no idea what he was up to. I don't know if they believe us, but we're going to play it safe for a while."

I breathe a sigh of relief that the repercussions weren't worse. "That's a good idea. I will too. There's so much I want to say, but I don't have time right now. Mentor Maxine said I could only have a few minutes in here."

"Does she know what you're doing?" Garth's voice sounds concerned.

"No."

"Okay, good. Please be careful. We need you, I—need you to be safe."

Did he really just say that? He cares about me! I didn't realize how much I needed to know that. "I need you to be safe too. Promise me you won't do anything stupid."

"I promise."

"Thanks for waiting for me, Garth. I've needed a kind voice all day."

"My voice is yours, any time you want it."

My stomach feels fluttery. "I-I wish I could talk to you every day, but we have to be careful. I'll write soon. Goodbye, Garth."

"Goodbye, Elira. Sweet dreams."

I tremble as I put the plexiglass back in place. I feel, so much better than I have all day. I stand up and wave to Garth as he smiles and waves back. Ahh. I will be okay. Like Mentor Maxine said, it's terrible to lose a friend, but my remaining friends will help me get through it. I smile at Mentor Maxine as I walk past her to my bedroom.

"Good night, Elira."

"Good night, Mentor Maxine."

Chapter 15

SHASTA SITS BY AVRA AND ME at morning victuals. She watches us closely but doesn't say anything. I am determined to be happy today. I'll start right now. "Hey, Shasta. Thanks for sitting by us. Did you sleep well?"

"Yeah, good enough. Vanessa kept sleep talking last night."

The image that brings to my mind is hilarious. "What did she say? Anything good?"

Shasta smiles mischievously. "She said something about you."

Avra nudges me and laughs out loud. "Well? What did she say?"

Shasta scoots her eggs around her tray. "At 9:45 she sat up in bed and yelled, 'Elira, I saw you meeting your five boys in the school room! Stop seeing them or I'll tell Mentor Roberta you're a dissident!' I shook her until she woke up. She was dead sure that you were meeting five boys in the school room though. I told her that Andric is gone so you couldn't meet with all five of them, even if you wanted to."

Avra starts to laugh, and I laugh with her to hide my discomfort. I was in the school room at 9:45 last night meeting Garth. Shasta doesn't mention that my bed was empty. I'm not going to bring it up. "Vanessa is desperate for some male attention, isn't she?" I ask. "She's even a jealous dreamer. I only get a tiny, little bit of boy attention."

Shasta folds her napkin after using it. "Yeah, it's funny. But while we are on the subject, you do get more than a tiny, little bit of attention, Elira. I think the whole glass dorm is mad that so many boys are trying to get you to look at them."

"I really don't ask for it."

"I know. I just worry that Vanessa or some other girl will do something mean to you out of jealousy."

I huff, "That's all I need." Shasta smiles at me sympathetically. I nod at her. "I'll try to ignore them more or be more discreet. Thanks, Shasta."

In the school room, I notice that Julie is smiling from ear to ear with Mara as I sit down in my usual seat. "Ow!" I jump out of my seat and pull a sewing pin out of my buttocks. Julie bursts out laughing. Mentor Bridget marches over to Julie and escorts her out of the room. I cringe as I sit down on my hard seat again—that pin went deep!

Mentor Bridget marches back into the school room and glares at us. "If any of the rest of you have stashed items from job research weeks, I suggest you turn them in or throw them away." She stares down Mara and a few other well-known troublemakers before continuing, "If I find one more pin, chemical, kitchen knife, or pair of scissors in this dorm that shouldn't be here, I will charge you as a dissident on the spot, so help me."

Vanessa raises her hand. "Has Julie been charged as a dissident?"

Mentor Bridget purses her lips. "No. She is on her absolute last warning though. The rest of you, consider this your last and final warning as well."

A murmur of disappointment flows through the room. I guess I'm not the only one who doesn't like Julie.

Mentor Bridget clears her throat. "Everyone, open your reading books to page 106 and read that short story. We will discuss it when you are done." Everyone stands up and gets a reading book off the shelf. Mentor Bridget meets me at the book shelf. "Are you okay, Elira?"

"Yeah, I'm fine."

"I've been harder on you than on Julie this last week, and I see now that it was a mistake to do that. I'm sorry."

"It's okay. I'm not very popular around here. I'm used to it."

"Well, after a day in a solitary cell, I'm sure Julie will think twice before she does something else."

"I hope you're right. Thanks."

I am thrilled when exploration time comes and Jefrey tries to communicate with me through the glass. When the other boys crowd around, I shake my head to steer them away. I remember Shasta's warning this morning. So just Jefrey and I smile and laugh as we try to communicate without sign language or papers. He points to his eye, so I think he's saying *I*. He lifts up his hand, and he's rubbing his fingers over his thumb back and forth. Hmm. I hear someone behind me mutter, "Money?" I turn around to see Mentor Bridget looking at Jefrey with a quizzical look on her brow. She sees me looking at her and turns and walks away.

I don't know what money has to do with anything. People use money to buy a spot in the complex, but we certainly don't use it in here. I think Jefrey might be saying feel. So *I feel...* I mouth the words then look to see what he does next. Jefrey holds up his hand again with his fingers sticking up and his thumb tucked in. Well, there are four fingers, does he mean four? *I feel four.* He is pointing at me now. *I feel four you*, or *I feel for you...* What? What does he feel for me? He points to his heart as the loud shriek sound goes off for victuals.

Shasta pulls me to the door for victuals even though I can't take my eyes off Jefrey's handsome face. "Lots of girls saw that, Elira. You didn't listen to me at all this morning, did you?"

"Y-yes. I did," I say even though my heart feels twice as big as my head right now. I don't care that Mara purposely steps on my foot during victuals, or that the guard stays in front of my window all night. This has been an amazing day, as far as I'm concerned.

Chapter 16

"ELIRA, I HAVEN'T SEEN YOU SMILE like this for weeks," Mentor Maxine says at morning victuals.

"Oh, well, I had a great day yesterday, and I think today will be a good one too," I say as my mind replays how Jefrey radiated as he touched his heart and looked at me yesterday.

"I hope it's still a great day after you learn the subject matter Mentor Bridget is teaching today." Mentor Maxine turns red and shakes her head.

"What are we learning about?"

"Uh, I don't really like talking about it. You'll just have to find out for yourself."

Curious why Mentor Maxine won't elaborate, I grab Avra's arm and walk into the school room, taking in every corner, hoping to figure out what uncomfortable learning is about to take place.

There are pictures of human bodies all over the walls. I'm pretty sure I've seen them in the doctor's office before. We're learning about the human body? What is so uncomfortable about that?

The older girls snigger and laugh as they look at the pictures on the walls. Shasta looks at me and smiles as she sits down. "I remember this day from last year. Have fun."

"If I have fun, you'll have fun too, right?"

Mentor Bridget clears her throat. "All of you 17 girls need to line up by the door. You've already had the lesson we're having today. There's no need to repeat it. Mentor Maxine will escort you all to the doctor's office." Shasta and Vanessa look nervous. Mentor Bridget calms them down. "Don't worry, you won't be getting a shot or an exam you have to get naked for. It's just your yearly check-up. One of our two doctors will check your eyes, ears, heart, and lungs. If one of the doctors finds that your deformities have worsened, you may have your button color changed. The doctor's office waiting room will be cramped with all of you going at once, so please use manners and decorum."

Without too much fuss, Shasta, Vanessa, and all the other older girls follow Mentor Maxine out the door.

Mentor Bridget sighs, "There now, having a smaller group makes this discussion easier." She hands each of us a pamphlet entitled, "How Babies are Made." Huh. I've always wondered how babies are made. This should be interesting. Avra raises her eyebrows at me and shrugs.

"I will give you sixty minutes to read the material in the pamphlet, and then we will discuss any questions that you have."

I hear gasps and giggles as the girls around me read the pamphlet. I feel my cheeks raise in temperature as I read it too. Avra leans over to me. "This is why they keep us separate."

"Yeah, I think so."

Mentor Bridget stands up to get our attention. "Okay, I know you learned a little bit about the hormones that cause your monthly cycles and draw males and females together in science a few years ago. This is the rest of the story about how we as human beings come to exist. I'm sure there are questions about what you've just read, so what are they?"

Mara raises her hand, "How often can a female have a baby? Every nine months, or do they wait longer to have another one?"

"Usually they wait longer to let the body heal before they have another one. Any other questions?"

Avra raises her hand and asks quietly, "How many babies do you think our mothers had before they died of the toxins?"

"It's different for each female. Some have internal

deformities, or lack of interest, or lack of opportunity to have children at all. Others have a child every year... until they die from the outside toxins. Every person is different, but because of the terrible effects of the toxins on human bodies, and limited complex space and food, it is becoming unpopular to have many children."

Jade raises her hand with a mischievous smile on her face. "So, have you ever, you know, tried to make a baby?"

Mentor Bridget turns beet red. "That is a personal question, not an academic question. I will not be answering it, and you will be scrubbing the toilets and showers in both bathrooms for your impertinence."

Jade groans and glares at the door. Okay, I guess that means we better keep this conversation academic.

Tessa shakes her short, black hair out of her eyes as she raises her skinny arm. "So, these things the pamphlet calls birth control really stop people from having babies?"

"Yes, they do."

Liza raises her hand forcefully. "I'm asking this question for academic reasons only. Will we ever get the chance to have a baby? Or will we always be separated from the boys by glass?"

"You will not ever have a baby, or even have the chance to. We only have so much room in the complex. You are lucky to have your spot and you have no money to pay for a child to have a spot."

Mara raises her hand again. "But, how will the human race survive?"

"There are people... who are healthier than you. They will make sure the human race survives. Do not tell yourself that human reproduction is your job. It is not. You have other equally important jobs to do. Most of you will always be separated from the boys. The few of you who will work with the boys at your future jobs will not share sleeping quarters with them or have any alone time with them. You don't want to pass on your deformities to a child, do you?"

Liza looks at her right hand that is missing a thumb. "Well, no, I don't, but I don't think the complex can stop everything nature intends."

"Actually, it can. It is not good for the survival of the human race to allow reproduction of extreme deformities."

My mind is positively exploding thinking about this. "So, you're saying that only people with minor or no deformities are allowed to have children."

"Yes. I am."

I blush as I ask, "I'm a yellow, why can't I?"

Mara scoffs out loud, "How many raccoon faces can this world handle?"

"That's enough, Mara." Mentor Bridget scratches her head in an agitated way. "If you live in this dorm, then you have 12 jobs to choose from. Having children is not one of them."

Liza pipes up, "Will the boys learn this stuff too?"

127

"Yes, they are learning it after noon victuals."

Avra is mortified, "That's going to make seeing Scott awkward," she says to me.

Liza raises her hand. "If the complex had a way to stop us from having babies with the boys, would they stop separating us?"

"They do have ways to stop you from having babies. It was tried many years ago, but the co-ed experiment was deemed a failure. Separation works better."

Jade glares at Mentor Bridget. "Some of us don't agree with that."

Mentor Bridget takes a deep breath. "It is a crazy, toxic world we live in, and we must all play our part if we want to survive. I don't have children because I am playing my part in the survival of the human race by being your school mentor. You will play your parts in the survival of the human race by growing food, cooking it, and keeping us clothed.

I raise my hand. "So what was the point of giving us this lesson, if we will never play a part in the creation of children?"

Avra pipes in. "I'm going to feel awkward when I see the boys through the glass from now on for no good reason."

Mentor Bridget looks at me thoughtfully before answering, "I have overheard many of you talking to each other about this subject. False information was being circulated. Knowledge makes us wiser when making choices in our jobs and more accepting of our place in the world than ignorance does." Okay… That's helpful, but not really.

I overhear Liza whispering to Jade, "This kind of knowledge just makes me want to try this stuff out."

I see Mentor Bridget write something on her clipboard before sending us out for noon victuals.

SHASTA GETS BACK from the doctor's office and sits with Avra and me for victuals. She has a smile on her face so big that I wonder how it all fits on her skinny face. "How was your baby lesson?"

Avra shakes her head and laughs. "Awkward."

I frown when I think about how much effort they take to keep us separate from the boys. "Yeah, I don't get why they want us to know, if we will never get to be near a boy."

Shasta shrugs. "Who knows. The doctor's office was crammed and horrible today."

"Did they change your button color?" I ask sarcastically.

"No, they don't come any darker than red. I sometimes think they'd give me a black button if they had one."

I take a quick sip of water. "Why do you say that?"

"They keep upping my pain and heart medication, and my spine keeps curving more. The looks on their faces don't give me much optimism."

"I know what you mean." Avra says.

I avoid the boys during exploration time because they are red-faced and still talking to their mentors about the baby pamphlet. Mentor Bridget helps Avra and me with our sign language alphabet. I was doing some of the letters wrong.

I do manage a wave to both Jefrey and Garth with minimal blushing before we're sent out of the school room for the night. As I crawl into bed, I wonder two things. One, will the guard ever leave my window during evening hours? Two, if I had the choice, would I want to have a baby?

Chapter 17

MENTOR MAXINE'S PURPLE BACK is the first thing I see as I crack open my eyes the next morning. What is she doing in here this early? I shut my eyes straight away, because it's blindingly bright, and I'm not ready to get up. Mentor Maxine isn't alone. I can hear someone else whispering. I strain my ears to pick up what is being said. "She is practically defunct, Maxine. We may as well send her to the final doctor now."

I'm pretty sure it's Mentor Roberta. I open my eyes just long enough to see Mentor Roberta folding her arms across her purple jumpsuit.

Mentor Maxine won't be bullied. "No, she has these spells from time to time, but she still has plenty of life left in her."

"But is she strong enough to work a job? If she's not, then we are wasting time and resources on a defunct worker. Keeping her is contrary to the whole point of this complex."

What the…

"I can't in good conscience send a reasonably healthy person to the death doctor."

"Don't think of them as people; think of them as what they really are: damaged, unpaid workers."

Gulp. Did I just hear that correctly? I don't think I can stomach any more of this conversation. I wiggle and squirm and pretend to wake up. The two mentors quit whispering. I look over at Avra's bed. She has an oxygen mask on and looks gray around the edges. Her eyes are closed.

"Is there a—*yawn* problem, Mentor Maxine?"

Mentor Maxine gives Mentor Roberta the evil eye as she answers me, "Yes Elira, there is. Avra isn't breathing well this morning."

"Oh, that happens to her from time to time, but she'll snap out of it before you know it. I'll keep an eye on her, so you can go about your day, if you like."

Mentor Maxine smiles at me and squeezes my shoulder. "Thank you, Elira. You are a good friend to Avra."

Mentor Roberta glares at Mentor Maxine and shakes her head. The mentors leave in an awkward silence. I fight the heavy feeling in my chest as I climb into Avra's bed and wrap my arms around her. Her curly black hair makes a soft pillow for me to lay on. Why does this have to happen right as I'm getting over Andric? I hold back my tears for a long time, but they start to leak out.

Vanessa yells at me from across the room, "I told you that sleeping by the window would make you sicker!"

I don't have to put up with this. "Shut up, you annoying know-it-all!" I hear Vanessa leaving in a huff, but I don't sit up to watch. I have got to do something. I can't let my best friend die.

I have this terrible feeling that Andric was right. We are all living a lie. I look at the girls across from me smiling and laughing as they make their beds. How can they be this happy, if the life we live is fake?

My waffling mind is suddenly set. My mission is to find out how deep the lie goes. Mentor Roberta made it sound like we are only here to be free labor. I need to know if that's true. My troubling observations are making more sense to me.

If this really is a labor complex... Avra probably won't be able to work full days, and they'll send her to the final doctor, or as Mentor Maxine put it, the death doctor. I won't let that happen. If it comes down to it, I will have to take Avra and break out of here. The toxic world can't be worse than imminent death.

How will I find out what I need to know? I will have to be

creative and question the mentors. No one else knows more than I do around here, well, except my boy gang.

Avra slowly wakes up. She wiggles weakly. "Elira, get off me. You're squishing me. Why are you crying?"

I sit up and wipe the tears from my puffy eyes. "I don't want you to die."

AVRA STAYS IN BED ALL DAY. I give her a pilfered pencil and piece of paper. She writes a note to Scott while I'm at morning classes.

I ask Mentor Bridget, "Do you mentors have a leader you follow, someone who makes the rules outside the complex?"

She says, "There isn't much left outside the complexes, but those of us who remain follow the leadership of Alexander Pristyne." That is all I can get from her. I'll have to try again later.

When I check on Avra before 12:00 victuals, I put the folded note she wrote for Scott in my pocket so I'll be ready to slip it through the grate when the opportunity arises.

"Are you feeling any better, Avra?"

She doesn't look like she'll be awake for long. "Yeah, a little."

"Keep resting. I'll take care of you." I kiss Avra on the forehead before I leave her.

I strategically place myself in the best viewing spot at the dining tables for 12:00 victuals. I want to know how the trays end up on the tables. Shasta sits by me, which I appreciate since Avra isn't leaving her bed today. I'm glad that Shasta accepted my apology about the shoot-out, and I think we're actual friends now. She watches me curiously, but doesn't ask me any questions.

A kitchen worker, dressed in a purple jumpsuit, comes through the door with a big, tall push cart full of aluminum food trays. The door clicks shut behind her. It must automatically lock. I'll have to test that theory later. She places a tray in front of every chair at the tables. She still has six slightly pinkish colored trays on her push cart. She just sits back and waits as people come in. Liza fluffs her red hair as she walks up to the food worker. The food worker takes one of the six pinkish trays off the cart and hands it to her.

I beckon Liza to join me at my table. She smiles and sits down next to me. She starts babbling about a boy I don't know. We pull the metal tops off our trays and start eating. Without being obvious, I examine Liza's tray. What is different about her tray than mine? I really can't tell. I stab a cube of chicken from her tray with my fork and pop it into my mouth. Mentor Maxine is immediately by my side.

"Don't eat Liza's food, Elira."

"Oh, sorry. She can have a bite of mine." I plop a chunk of chicken from my tray into Liza's tray.

Liza glares at me, stands up, and moves to another table. Shasta finishes her last bite and leaves too. Uh, awkward.

Mentor Maxine looks at me cautiously as she lowers her voice. "It's not a matter of portion control, Elira. Liza is being... medicated for a condition she has. You don't want to ingest her medicine. The medicated trays just started today, and more girls will probably start getting them."

My eyebrows knit themselves together. "The medicine is mixed into her food?"

Mentor Maxine speaks in a whisper, "Yes. The complex management thinks you girls will purposely not take your medicine if we hand it out as pills to swallow, so it is mixed into the food. This is classified information, so don't tell anyone. I just don't want you to get... hurt."

"Liza seems pretty healthy. What is the medicine for?"

"I can't tell you. Watch the six girls who received special trays today. What do they have in common?" Mentor Maxine walks away quickly before I can ask another question.

During exploration time, and much to Jefrey's dismay, I finally finish my drawings of the sign language alphabet. I'm pretty sure that the mysterious woman with the black curly hair and pale skin signed C and K to me over a week ago. I can't quite remember the other letters, an O? Or a J or a Y perhaps? Oh well, I'll figure it out if she shows up tonight. I don't care if it takes all night for the guard to leave. I will stay up to get any answers the woman can offer. I just hope the guard at my window hasn't scared her off forever.

There is about five minutes left of exploration time. Jefrey, Garth, and Rocky are standing by the grate. I wonder where Bryon is—oh, I see him sitting at a desk working on the extra credit problems. That's kind of weird that he is working on the problems by himself. Oh, well. I walk slowly to the three boys in the corner. The news I have to share isn't good. It's depressing, really. The boys stare intently at me, trying to decipher my somber mood. Their mood has been darker too, since the loss of Andric. I don't look into the twins' eyes for very long, because I don't want my heart to start racing.

Whack. A girl with black spikey hair plows into me. I hit the glass wall with a *thud.* I barely stay on my feet. A loud girl fight breaks out near the corner. One girl with blonde curly hair is pulling the black spikey-haired girl's hair and that girl slaps her attacker's arms. She eventually gets in the right position to connect a slap to her face. They break apart for a second and now there are two groups of girls facing each other down, screaming at each other. It sounds like it's over the curly blonde girl trying to kiss a boy through the glass. Ew. I don't really care; I just hope they keep all eyes in the room on them instead of me.

I kneel down by the grate cover and twist it up. The sound barrier pops out with a tug. I slide the note from Avra through a slot on the boys' side. Jefrey sinks down to his knees and sticks a note halfway through a slot. I take it. The other two boys are blocking the view of what he is doing. Another note pokes through, and then another. I take them all.

"Jefrey?"

"Yes? I'm here."

Sigh. He is right on the other side of that thin piece of metal. "The note I gave you is for Scott from Avra. I didn't have time to write, but I have lots to tell you guys."

"Oh, I was hoping the note was for me. You look sad. Are you still sad about Andric?"

"Yes and no. There's too much to bring up now, but they just started medicating some of the girls' victuals. The medicated trays are pinkish."

Rocky's voice is quiet, but I can hear it from above. He must be eaves dropping. "Oh no. Bryon ate a tray that was blueish today."

Jefrey leans his forehead against the metal plate. "I wondered why he was acting different this afternoon."

"Help me figure out what the people they are medicating have in common. I have to go. Bye, Jefrey."

"Bye, Elira."

I try not to let the tingles I feel slow me down as I put the plexiglass back in place. I slide the cold air return cover back to where it should be as Mentor Maxine storms over to break up the fight.

The loud shriek sound goes off. It's time for 5:00 victuals.

I wave at the boys as I hurry to the dining area before anyone notices how much time I spent with them. I sit in the same seat that allows me to see who is eating from which trays.

I really don't know much about the first girl who gets a pink tray. She's a year older than me, and I've never talked to her. The second girl to get one is Liza. I know her, of course. The third girl is Liza's friend, Jade. The fourth is the older girl with the curly blonde hair that caused the fight today, and the fifth and final tray is given to the black spikey-haired girl. I thought Mentor Maxine said there were six, hmmm.

Chapter 18

I RUSH TO MY ROOM after I'm done eating to read my notes. Avra is sitting up in her bed eating out of a pink tray. Ahh!

"Avra! You can't eat that! The pink trays are medicated!"

"Uh, what am I supposed to eat? You know the rules, if you refuse your tray, you starve."

"I know that, but this is not good. What are we going to do? The complex is trying to do something to us. I'm not sure what yet, but something!"

"Why would you say that? The complex keeps us safe from the toxins!"

141

I sit down on her bed and lower my voice. "Avra, I know this may sound crazy, but I need you to trust me. I heard the mentors talking about you this morning. You looked bad, like you wouldn't get better, ever, bad."

"Okay, so?"

"Mentor Roberta wants to send you to the 'death doctor' because she doesn't think you're strong enough for a job. She said that's all we're here for, free labor!"

Avra frowns at me. "I've been to both complex doctors tons of times, there is no death doctor."

"Well, obviously you haven't been to him, because no one comes back from there!"

"Get off my bed, Elira!" My usually sweet friend pushes me off her bed. *Thump.* She glares at me as I raise myself off the floor. "My head hurts, and I need to lie down." Avra turns away from me as she lays her head on the pillow.

I dust myself off with determination. "The final doctor is the death doctor, Avra." I want to scream and shake her. This is my best friend; why won't she believe me?

Avra's voice is muffled by her pillow. "I think you were half-asleep when you supposedly heard all this. It doesn't make sense!"

Okay, we are getting nowhere. I'll try again later. "Take a nap, Avra. Dream of Scott and then you'll be ready to have this conversation with me."

"Why would I dream of Scott? That's stupid. I'd rather dream of chocolate cake, *yawn*. Good night."

Oh… It finally clicks. All the girls who were given pink trays today are boy crazy. I can't believe Avra, who spent all morning writing a love letter to Scott, doesn't want to dream about him. What kind of medicine did they give her? Whatever it is, it's working. I wonder if the boys have any new information in their letters. I plop down on my bed. I pull out the letter addressed to me from Garth. I hope it contains something I want to hear. I look around to see if anyone is watching me. The coast is clear. With trembling hands, I open it up.

Dear Elira,

I can't believe how much you have helped us. Breaking into the cold air return was pure genius. I had a feeling we could communicate through it. Andric tried several different things that stripped the screw heads on our side. I don't know why none of us ever tried using a spoon as a screwdriver. It could be a game changer if we are careful and use it right. The complex has gotten away with its secrets because we've all been completely happy to obey the rules and not communicate with each other about things that matter.

It helped me to talk to you about Andric the other day. It's been hard pretending like I'm not screaming inside every time someone talks about him. I want to communicate with you, Elira. If I had enough paper, I would write to you every day. Honestly, I can't get the sound of your voice out of my head, no matter what I do. Talk or write to me every chance you get. I want to know everything about you. I've missed looking into your eyes lately. It seems like you're learning sign language. We have a red button guy on our side who can't hear. I know a little bit of sign language. If you're learning it, then I will improve mine, so we can communicate through the glass better.

With Andric gone, Rocky has been scheming and dreaming like crazy. He has some pretty intense theories about what is really going on in the complex. He is my best friend, and I think that at least some of his ideas are right. You see the fakeness going on around here. I can tell that you aren't satisfied with this little boxed-in life we have. You wouldn't have broken into the grate if you were. It is dangerous to do what we're doing. Make sure you flush all our letters down the toilet. If any of them are found, we could be charged as dissidents, like Andric. I will be at the cold air return tomorrow night at 8:00. Meet me there, please.

I will try to pilfer paper every chance I get. If you see the big bald mentor who wears a green jumpsuit on our side, don't do anything to compromise yourself. He is watching us. He would be glad to charge any of us as dissidents.

Until next time,

Garth

Wow. My hands caress the crinkly letter written on cast-off homework paper. It represents some harsh realities that I haven't considered, but it also represents a boy who can't get my voice out of his head! I don't think I can flush this letter down the toilet...

I see Garth's face in my mind. He misses looking into my eyes, even though one of them is ugly and purple. I smell the paper, hoping to catch any scent from Garth. I can smell the tiniest whiff of something. It's the opposite of the fruity and flowery scents I've smelled on my mentors. I think it's the scent of manliness. I fold the letter back up and stuff it under my mattress. I open the letter from Rocky next.

Elira,

Thank you for the information you've gleaned from your mentors and especially the news of a woman outside the complex. I have seen two different people through the windows of the complex. I'm pretty sure that this mysterious woman is one of them. I noticed that neither of the people I've seen out there appear sick. They seem to be healthy and not struggling to survive at all. Last year when we had a window, the woman tried to communicate with us even though she was chased off by the guards every time.

I have a theory. I know this may not be easy to believe, but I think we are living one big, giant lie. I don't think the outside world is toxic. We now know that the mentors leave the complex to their own apartments when their shifts are over. I don't think they put on thick, impenetrable guard suits when they leave. I think they just walk out the door with skin showing, and they probably laugh, because they've tricked us all into believing the big lie for one more day.

I'm tired of the lie, Elira. I want to get out of here. I have one memory of my life before the complex. My parents tried to keep me. I remember my mother crying and screaming when they took me away. I think my parents are still alive out there. In fact, I know they are. I feel it in my bones. Will you help me figure out a way to escape this complex? I have tried everything I can think of over here. I need some new ideas.

I keep getting the feeling that the answer lies on your side of the glass. You are smart and have already proven yourself very useful. Will you keep helping me?

Don't tell anyone about this plan. Destroy all evidence of our letters.

Keep your eyes open,
Rocky

Whoa. Lies, lies, lies! I've known there are lies circling around this place, but, no toxins? Either the mentors are lying to me, or Rocky is. I read the letter from Rocky one more time and memorize all the important information, then crumble it into a ball. I shakily rush to the bathroom, lock myself in a stall and flush the letter down the toilet. I sit on the toilet fully clothed, and put my head in my hands. I knew there was something amiss about this place, but can the lie we're living be THAT big? Do I have parents out there, fully healthy, wishing they could get me out of this thick-walled complex? How do I find out? *Flush.*

Great, someone is in here. Where is Mentor Maxine when I need her? I stand up and flush the toilet one more time. My hands fumble as I try to unlock the stall. Get a grip on yourself, Elira. Don't let anyone know you are a dissident. At the row of sinks, I see Liza washing her hands in a blank, detached way.

I force a smile on my face as my raccoon eye stares back at me in the mirror. "Hey, Liza. Thanks for asking that cute boy of yours to get Garth last night in the school room."

Liza looks at me like she's disgusted by my words. "I don't have a cute boy. Boys are not cute. Excuse me, I have to go organize my drawers." She slams the door as she leaves the bathroom.

Water splashes onto the floor as my hands start to shake again. The mirror in front of me reveals a ghost with pale white

147

skin and a purple eye. That was not the Liza of yesterday. I knew it. The medicated victuals in the pink trays are for all the boy-crazy girls. The medicine makes them stop liking boys.

Why would they want that? I remember the 'How Babies are Made' pamphlets and the girl fight I witnessed earlier. That sparks something Mentor Roberta said to Mentor Maxine when Avra wasn't breathing well. The whole point of the complex is to have damaged, unpaid workers. Slapping and hair-pulling isn't the best way to get a job done, is it?

I rush back into my stall. I'm going to be sick. My stomach holds nothing back. The gurgle of the porcelain toilet mocks me as I leave my stall.

I pinch my cheeks to put some color into my white face when Mentor Bridget storms in. She dumps a bunch of old school papers into the garbage can before she trots to a stall. I smile half-heartedly at her as she passes me. Ooh, paper, I need that. I turn the sink on full blast as I pilfer the top half of the papers out of the garbage can and shove them down the front of my jumpsuit. I turn off the water and rush to my room.

No one but sleeping Avra is in here, thank goodness. I stuff all but one of the papers under my mattress and write down everything I have pieced together about the complex. Mentor Maxine is right. It is helpful to get other points of view about what you're studying. What are the chances that I can get into the school room grate twice in one day?

Mentor Maxine comes rushing by, supporting a green-faced girl with one arm. "Elira, I need a huge favor. Tessa just threw up in the school room, is there any way you could clean it up for me? I don't dare leave Tessa's side."

Hmm, I hope it's nerves and not the flu that kept me in the bathroom earlier. On the bright side, this is exactly what I need. "Yeah, I will. I will find you when I'm done."

"Thank you, Elira."

As I enter the school room, squeals of laughter bombard my ears. Two girls are sharing the telephone to talk to a boy on the other side of the glass. Their cleaning rags are all but forgotten on the floor. Another girl is pressing a letter to the glass. I'm surprised to see that it's Rocky who reads it from the other side. He winks at me. I lift the edge of my letter out of my pocket, so he can see it. He nods. The girl thinks it's approval for her, but I know it's affirmation for me. The sour-smelling mess that has almost cleared the room is next to the garbage can, which is near the corner I need to get to.

Sterile gloves slap against my wrists as I pull them on, the other cleaning supplies I need are easily found in the janitor closet. It doesn't take long to clean the barf up. The girls by the window keep plugging their noses and frowning at me. Get over yourselves. I am improving the smell. I double bag the garbage and tie a big knot on the bundle. I will take it out shortly. If I place the garbage can and the bag in a line, they block the view of what I am doing, mostly.

Scritch, scratch, the metal grate cover whines as I twist it up. The girls by the phone start jumping up and down, oohing and ahhing. Huh? I kneel up to see what they are looking at through the glass. Rocky is doing flips and somersaults for some reason. What a distraction he can be. Oh yeah, duh. I crouch down and swing the grate cover up again. I make record time popping out the sound barrier and dropping the note through a metal grate crack. As I fit everything back into place, I hear *Tap, tap, tap* right behind me.

The foot tapping freezes me in place. An unpleasant voice asks, "What are you doing, Elira?"

I spin around to see Julie glaring at me.

"Oh-oh goody, you're back from isolation," I stammer like a stuttering child. "I-I just cleaned up barf for Mentor Maxine."

Her smile is anything but kind. "Oh, I think we both know you did more than that." Julie walks over to the grate cover and swings it up. To my ears, the *creak, scritch, scratch, thump* sounds like the last nail going into my coffin.

Julie smugly backs up toward the door. "I'm sure Mentor Maxine will have a few words to say about this."

Oh good. Mentor Maxine is on duty. I make sure my relief doesn't show. I fake panic, "No! Please don't tell Mentor Maxine, Julie."

"Oh, I am telling her all right. I bet you wish you hadn't poured water down my front, smashed pie in my face, and stolen both of the twins, don't you?"

Uh, nope. But I have to look distraught. I pull on my hair.

"You're right! I shouldn't have done any of that. Please don't tell."

Julie smirks as she leaves the room. "Too late."

I can't help but smile as I go back to pick up the garbage bag.

I'M SO LUCKY it was Mentor Maxine and not Mentor Roberta who handed out my punishment. Thank goodness Mentor Maxine likes me, because my punishment is doing something I want to do anyway. I wonder if she knows what I'm up to... The screws are put back in the grate cover and I am assigned a day in the dirty laundry room. The letter from Jefrey is not found in my pocket. Rocky picked up his letter before anyone saw it. It will be okay, by some miracle.

I collapse on my bed after accepting my punishment. It has been the most emotionally exhausting day I've ever had. Luckily, I know what will make me feel better. I pull Jefrey's letter out of my pocket and smell it. It smells different than Garth's. Sweeter, maybe? I need some sweetness right about now. I hope this does the trick.

Dear Elira,
I think you are the cutest girl in the whole complex. I don't

think your purple eye mask diminishes your beauty at all. In fact, I feel like we have matching marks. Do you think we match?

I'm glad you're part of our gang now, but you might want to take everything my brother and Rocky say with a grain of salt. They think the world isn't toxic, and that we should escape the complex. Think about it though, if they are wrong and we march outside without protective suits, we are goners. I can't bear the thought of you suffering in any way.

Will you meet me at the grate privately some time? I want to hear your voice again so badly. Wear your black jumpsuit, it looks good on you.

I will see you later, through the glass.

Jefrey

He wants to meet me privately! That sends my heart racing. Does this letter thrill me more than Garth's did? I can't tell. When I'm done memorizing the letter, I stuff it under my mattress.

I turn off the lamp by my bed. Avra is asleep, and I think everyone else is too. The guard is in front of my window like usual. I can wait him out. I slip into bed and watch the window. Right as I'm about to doze off I notice the guard shifting away from the glass. I slip out of bed and look out the window. The guard's head is bent over. He is snoozing. What luck! He suddenly jerks his head up, and I duck down so he won't see me if he turns around. He doesn't turn around; he walks ten feet to the right. He leans against the wall and droops his head again. He can't see me at all, even if he's awake.

I look to the tree line. Eyes! Oh good. The mysterious woman sticks her head out of the gap in the trees and waves. I wave back. I sign *Hi, I am Elira.* She picks up a rock and waves it at me again. I wish I knew what that meant.

She then signs, *Do you know my son? R-O-C-K-Y.*

Chapter 19

FIRST THING IN THE MORNING I run to the school room and sign up for the telephone before anyone is done with their victuals. I need to tell Rocky that the mysterious woman is his mother. I want to tell him with my actual voice if I can. If he has any doubts about escaping the complex, he won't after he hears my news. His mom is right outside the complex walls! I wish mine was.

As I plop my last gooey bite of oatmeal into my mouth, the loud shriek noise goes off. That's weird, we just finished our victuals. It must be a special announcement. I move to the other side of the common room and sit on one of the soft, white sofas before they're all taken. Tessa and Shasta join me. Avra squeezes in next to me as well. Ow, she's sitting on half my leg.

I hope my recent activities have nothing to do with this important announcement. This kind of thing doesn't happen often. Mentor Maxine waits for everyone to gather into the common room, then pulls out an official-looking letter and reads it loud enough for all of us to hear.

"Attention complex dwellers: today is administration inspection day. The administration of the complex will be inspecting every corner of the complex to make sure everything is in proper working order, and that residents are being treated correctly. Our number one goal is to keep you safe from the toxins outside. If you have any concerns about the complex, you may address the complex chief during exploration time today. Please line up in an orderly manner. The chief will address as many of you as he can in the time allotted.

Phew, at least it isn't about me or my gang. I wish today was my laundry duty day instead of tomorrow. I don't like administration inspection days. They happen twice a year, and everyone is always super proper and quiet and boring. Woohoo. I always feel uncomfortable watching the administration writing on their clipboards every second of the day.

Mentor Maxine corners me when she's done talking to everyone. "Elira, don't even look at your boys today, do you hear me?" The concern in her eyes is pouring out faster than she can hold it back.

"Why?"

A weary sigh escapes her lips. "Everyone in this complex asks me how, where, when, what, but you are the only one who ever asks me why." Mentor Maxine seems pleased, yet anxious. "You are an amazing young woman, Elira. You notice things. You can tell when something isn't right. I am incredibly proud that you are this way, but today you need to act like everyone else."

I grab her arm before she can walk away. "You still haven't answered my question. Why?"

Mentor Maxine's voice drops to barely a whisper, "The administration is looking specifically for dissidents today. On both sides of the glass. Don't do anything that will jeopardize you or your friends. I have to go pretend I am the administration's lap dog. I suggest you do the same." She walks off quickly.

Huh. As much as I want to tear this place apart to figure out how to escape, I can wait. I won't jeopardize myself or my friends. As I walk past the empty tables on my way to the school room, I do a quick counting. There are 12 empty pink trays today instead of six. I guess more girls are being noticeably boy crazy. I wonder why I don't have a pink tray. As Vanessa says, I do hang out with more than my fair share of boys. I bet Mentor Maxine is keeping them from medicating me.

My goal for the day is to stay as close to the administration as I can, without being obvious, so I can glean as much information as possible.

As the empty trays are cleaned up by the workers from the kitchens, the Complex Chief walks into the glass dorm. The happy babble of the dorm turns to silence. He exudes an air of superiority and dissatisfaction. The Complex Chief is tall and broad-shouldered with an unusually thin waist and scrawny legs. His face is long and thin, and his straight black hair looks like it was cut with a ruler and scissors around his crown and stuck to his head with glue. The yellow-toothed sneer on his face makes me want to either look down at my feet, or stare at him in horror so I don't miss who he pounces on first.

He looks us all over and immediately starts writing on his clipboard. He has a pretty, blonde assistant with him and she follows him around smiling at the room in general without getting too close to him.

I cautiously follow him around too. Mentor Maxine opens her eyes as wide as they'll go and shakes her head almost imperceptibly at me. She knows what I'm trying to do. Fine. I'll just sit here and do nothing all day.

When we move into the school room for morning classes, Avra lays her head down on her arms. Today must not be a good day for her. That is unfortunate. The Complex Chief looks at her then whispers with Mentor Bridget. I get up to grab a piece of paper. I overhear him say, "If she can't be consistent in her schooling then she won't be consistent in a job. We are behind schedule in 8 out of 12 production sectors, we need to cut the fat and become a lean, mean, productive machine."

"Maxine thinks she is healthy enough to be reasonably productive in a chair. That's the only reason we haven't sent her to the final doctor."

"If she hasn't proven her work ethic by the end of the month, send her to the doctor."

"Yes, Chief."

Oh boy. One month. I've got to get her out of here. But how? There has to be a way. I trudge back to my seat. I don't think I can fake a smile all day long. I hope this jerk leaves our dorm soon. I bury myself in my school work.

After noon victuals and math, Mentor Bridget looks excited about the change to our usual schedule. "Exploration time, girls. Today you may ask the Complex Chief one question about any complex concerns you have. Line up in an orderly manner and keep your questions short."

Vanessa immediately jumps out of her seat and starts the front of the line. Mara is right behind her. She twists her long white-blonde hair around a finger on her shriveled hand. She seems nervous for once.

I try to decide if I should ask the Complex Chief one of my many questions. Mentor Maxine won't like it; I'm supposed to be blending in. But how often do I get to ask the head honcho of this place any question I want? I haven't looked at my boys even once. I haven't asked any off the wall questions. I've been sitting here good as gold. Surely, I can risk one tiny little question. Shasta stands up and gets in the line. Wow, I am surprised by that. I let my heart instead of my head guide me as I join Vanessa, Mara, and Shasta in the line. I don't really know what I'm going to ask yet. But I'm sure it will come.

Vanessa smiles at the Complex Chief in her awkward way and asks, "Why don't you reseal the window edges every six months? I have noticed the people near the window get sick more than everyone else, and I personally don't want to absorb any extra toxins."

The Complex Chief purses his lips together while he thinks and then opens his mouth so we can see his horrible yellow teeth. "It would be a waste of government money to reseal the windows every six months. We always make sure the windows get new caulk every January, before everyone moves dorms. That is a normal and acceptable space of time between sealings. Do not fear the outside toxins from within the complex. It is our job to keep you safe, and we do that job well."

Vanessa does not look impressed as she sits down. Julie jumps up and gets in line behind me. She *accidentally* bumps into my back in the process. "Sorry, mask-face." If the complex chief was not here right now, I would seriously punch her in the face.

Mara steps forward, straightens herself, looks the Complex

Chief in the eye, and asks her question, "Why do we have to share the glass dorm with two age groups? We've never had to share a dorm with this many girls before, and I feel like the drama and fighting would be much less if we didn't have as many girls living together."

The Complex Chief looks like he is going to die of boredom with this question. His voice is monotone and unenthusiastic as he responds, "There is wisdom in combining two age groups into one dorm. Job preparation is the main reason. If you can't get along with 60 girls, how will you get along with five times that many on the job? I suggest you enjoy sharing a dorm with only 60." The Complex Chief looks down at his clipboard. "Oh, make that 59 girls. When you turn 18, you will share a dorm with all the girls that work with you. If you do not think you can handle those kinds of living conditions, let your mentors know. They can provide you with... supplements to make the transition easier for you. Next question."

Shasta impresses me with her determination as she takes a step forward. "Why can reds only apply for four jobs? I really want to be a guard, but I feel like I have no choice but to be a cook or something even less appealing to me."

The complex chief keeps his eyes down as he scribbles something on his clipboard. "We take the health of all complex residents very seriously. Red workers are very valuable in the kitchens and in the laundry, but we cannot risk the loss of life that would come from putting reds in high-risk jobs. It's not safe for the red, and it's not safe for those who work alongside the red. I would personally feel less safe knowing all the guards who protect this complex day in and day out were suffering from heart, lung, and eye problems. Next question." Shasta lowers her head dejectedly and sits back down.

It's my turn. I step forward, "Complex Chief, I understand why the boys and girls in the complex have to stay separate, but aren't we missing critical points of view by not learning together? One telephone for over 100 people does not help us to gather much academic information from each other."

The Chief looks at me long and hard before answering. "This is a government facility. The government pays for everything that happens here. The government does not want the degenerate genes of this demographic to be replicated. In order to ensure no degenerate genes are replicated we must keep all parties interested in reproduction either separated or medicated. There is time to collaborate in certain jobs that benefit from multiple points of view. Thank you, that's all the time I have." The Chief stands up and leaves the room. I walk back to my seat dejectedly.

Avra lifts her head up. "What in the world did that mean?" The other girls who listened in all shrug and shake their heads before heading off to 5:00 victuals.

I wait for the Chief's blonde aid to follow him out. I lean close to Avra. "It means, the government thinks we're damaged and doesn't want us to pass our damaged genes on to a new generation. They keep girls and boys separate so that we don't have babies. Now that it is time to start working with each other, anyone who wants a boyfriend will be medicated. Our deformities are supposed to die with us."

"But everyone in the world is deformed in some way. Everyone knows that."

I lower my voice and say forcefully, "Or we have been told that, and we've believed it. Things are not good here, Avra. We are being lied to. We have to escape."

Avra glares at me. "You are crazy, Elira. I am not strong enough to escape."

"You have to be. I heard the chief say that if you don't prove you are strong enough for a job by the end of the month, you're going to the death doctor. You are a waste of government money to him."

Avra squirms in her seat. "I don't believe it. You need to quit listening to your crazy boys. They are nothing but trouble."

"That's not what you said a few days ago. You have to stop eating the food in your pink tray. I'll share my food with you."

"You are getting crazier and crazier, Elira. I need to rest. Leave me alone." Avra turns away from me and lays her head on her desk.

I turn around and look at the glass wall. The bald mentor is in the room, but he has his back turned to the window as he helps a boy with his schoolwork.

Garth and Rocky are looking right at me. I discreetly turn my back so Mentor Bridget can't see what I'm doing in front of my chest. I have so much to say, and not much time to say it. I use my hands to spell out, "Big problems. Chief looking for dissidents. Avra is going to death doctor soon. Rocky's mom…"

I guess Rocky knows sign language too, because he jumps up and runs to the glass window. He braces his hands against it, as soon as I spell out "Rocky's mom". I see his mouth screaming the words, "What about my mom? Do you know where my mom is?" Just then, I notice that the chief is inside the boys' school room. The chief talks to the bald mentor who grabs Rocky and hauls him out of the room.

Oh no. What have I done?

Chapter 20

AS THE SKY TURNS DARK, I don't even try to look out my window, my pillow swallows my heavy head instead. I've sent Rocky's life down the toilet. I know Rocky's mom is outside right now, but I don't want anyone else to get caught trying to communicate with me. I feel a tear leak out of my eye and slowly roll down the side of my face. It absorbs into my hair. I feel a waft of air touch the cold wet line on my face as someone kneels down beside my bed.

"I told you not to look at any of them," Mentor Maxine whispers.

The single wet line on my cheek is joined by many more

as I roll to my side. "It's all my fault. What is going to happen to him?"

Mentor Maxine lets out a long breath. "He is in a private cell being forcibly medicated right now. If it doesn't change him, he will be charged as a dissident and sent to the final doctor."

"Who is really the death doctor." I wipe the tears off my purplish eye.

Mentor Maxine cocks her head to the side. "Yes... how do you know that?"

I don't know if I should tell her, but I really want to. "I overheard you and Mentor Roberta the other day." I glare at the ceiling. "How is he being forcibly medicated?"

Mentor Maxine gently slides a stray piece of hair behind my ear. "He refuses to eat the medicated food, so he is being injected with the medicine."

"Being girl-crazy isn't really his problem, you know."

"What do you think his problem is?"

I look at Mentor Maxine and try to decipher if she is as trustworthy as I think she is. "Will you turn me in if I tell you?"

Mentor Maxine leans closer to me and whispers, "No. I won't. I'm on your side. I just want to know how much you two know."

My voice cracks. "He told me that all of this is a lie."

Mentor Maxine gets up from her knees and sits on the side of my bed. I scoot over to make room for her. She looks at me full of sympathy. "I figured as much. He has been watched for quite a while. Mentor Briggs was just waiting for him to do something stupid in front of the complex chief to charge him as a dissident. So, it really isn't your fault. They were going to take him away sooner or later."

"Am I being watched?"

Mentor Maxine's voice is soft. "Yes."

"What should I do?"

"What does your gut tell you to do?"

"It tells me to break out of here and to bring Avra and my boy gang with me."

Mentor Maxine looks around the room before saying into my ear, "I think that would be wise."

Surprised, I wipe the wet tear tracks off my face and sit up. "Really?"

Maxine inches closer to me, "The complex chief took your question as a sign of overheated femaleism. He wanted to start you on pink trays tomorrow. I convinced him to start you on the medicated trays in a week instead."

Wow—I thought I'd have a month to figure all this out. Instead, the time is now. "Thank you for looking out for me. Are you going to get in trouble, Maxine? Is it okay if I call you that?"

"You may when we're in private. I worry that I am being watched as well. My suggestions for resident rights are sending red flags. You shouldn't tell me your plans in case they interrogate me. I'll help you as much as I can without being obvious."

"What will happen to you?"

"I may lose my job, but they can't hurt me. I am a hearty working citizen. I have rights."

"But I don't."

"…I'm afraid not."

"What will the world do to me when I break out? Will they bring me back?"

Maxine tilts her head back and forth as if deciding. "Yes. They probably will bring you back. You'll have to live in hiding. I wish your birthmark was somewhere you could cover. A break out will be big news. Your face will give you away in a second."

"Do you have any deformities?"

"No."

"So, is it true that no one has any deformities out there?"

Maxine rubs her forehead and sighs. "Almost no one. All children with deformities are brought here. When a child turns two, they must undergo a thorough examination. If there is anything physically or mentally wrong with them, they are brought here. A few parents go rogue and hide their children. But they are caught. Every time. Some people have accidents as adults, but not very many. All the dangerous jobs are done here. If one of you loses a hand in a machine, oh well. You were damaged anyway."

I sit up and look out the window. The world just got bigger. "Where will I go when I break out?"

"I don't know. I guess you can stay at my apartment until you decide what to do."

I breathe a sigh of relief. "Thank you, Maxine. Do you think—there is any chance my parents will take me back?"

Maxine nods hesitantly. "If they are alive, I think so. Only cruel, horrible parents are happy to see their children go, no matter what is wrong with them." Maxine stands up. "Make good use of your time in the laundry room tomorrow. I have to go."

I GET UP EARLY THE NEXT MORNING and watch all the girls eat their victuals. Anyone who doesn't eat something off a normal tray, I swipe what they leave behind. I sneakily offer to get Avra her tray. Oops! I pull off the top and *accidentally* spill most of it onto the floor. Mentor Roberta yells at me and is too angry to think straight when she tells me that I have to give Avra my tray. No problem. That's what I wanted to do anyway. Avra grumbles and grouches at me as I give her my victuals. She claims that the pink trays taste sweeter. I'm not surprised; these people are tricky. Shasta rolls her eyes at me when I sit down trayless. She gives me her peaches. Tessa pats my hand and gives me her eggs. I successfully glean enough food to get by for myself.

Laundry day is here at last. I hope my mind has enough fuel to take mental notes of everything I see today. Mentor Roberta personally escorts me to the laundry room once I finish eating. As we exit the glass dorm door, I expect a world of wonder to open up to me. Instead, I'm greeted by dim, dingy hallways that stretch out before me in several directions. Mentor Roberta silently scowls at me as she closes the door to the glass dorm and locks it behind me. *Click.* She puts the key in her side pocket. The only sounds my hungry ears hear are Mentor Roberta's loud sniffing and our footsteps echoing off the gray floors and walls. *Tap, tap, tap.*

Every gray door we pass looks exactly like the last one except for its shiny gold number. The numbers increase as we proceed down the first hall, but when we take a right turn, the numbers start to decrease. Confusing! I'm sure I couldn't find my way back on my own, but I will try to memorize the path back when I leave. I had no idea that this complex was so big, and so maze-like. We make several more turns and go down some stairs before we reach the laundry room.

A strong soapy scent overwhelms my nostrils as I enter the enormous room. I'm shocked to see at least 100 people in dark-brown jumpsuits rushing to and fro in here. I never dreamed that so many people were taking care of my laundry each day. The hum of 30 washers and 30 dryers get louder the farther in we walk. I am going deaf I realize as Mentor Roberta asks me a question that I can't decipher. We walk around a corner to a soaking tub for jumpsuits that are heavily soiled. There is a folding station and a sorting section beyond this area, but it doesn't look like I get to check it out.

It's quieter here, thank goodness. Mentor Roberta tells the laundry advisor that since I am being punished, I should have the dirtiest, smelliest jobs that she can give me. I am taken to the chute room. My jaw drops in awe as I witness clothes dropping from 50 or more circle chutes in the ceiling into massive tubs. Dirty sorters then sort the dirty clothes into 5 different smaller, wheeled bins: whites, lights, darks, heavily soiled, and trash.

I ask the head sorter, "Why do you need trash bins down here?"

"Good question, young lady. Some complex dwellers think it is funny to send trash down the laundry chute."

"Oh, rude."

"Plus some clothing gets too soiled or too ripped to be salvageable, so that is sent out with the trash as well."

I lean over one of the giant tubs to see what's in the bottom of it. It has white bras and underwear of all sizes mixed with jumpsuits and bedding. *Plop*. Something lands on my head. I shake my head in horror to dislodge whatever it is. It looks like underwear, but bigger and blockier. "What is that?"

The sorter next to me picks it up off the floor and puts it back in the whites bin. "Boy underwear."

171

"Gross." I shake my head again as though the underwear is still there.

The head sorter chuckles and pushes a heavily soiled bin at me. A waft of nasty odor hits me in the face as I grab it. Ew. Did all this laundry come from the kids who aren't potty-trained yet? I am not touching any of this multicolored stinkiness with my bare hands. The head sorter nods at the wall. I take a pair of gloves out of a box on the wall before I wheel the bin over to the soaking tub. I take a paddle sticking out of the soaking tub and use it to lift the heavily soiled jumpsuits, bedding, and underwear out of the wheeled bin and into the soaking tub. I use the paddle to push the dry clothes down to the bottom of it.

The head soaking-tub attendant approaches me. "Hi. I'm Rebecca. You need to constantly stir the tub. Okay, missy?"

I rub my raccoon eye distractedly. "Okay."

I try not to gag or make noises as I examine the heavily soiled items I'm supposed to save from the nastiness. Mentor Roberta smiles at my discomfort at first, but after an hour she loses interest in me and goes back to the glass dorm. It's about time. I need to find out the secrets of this place. I cozy up to Rebecca now that I'm not being watched.

"So, tell me. When do I get the next batch?"

Rebecca is a wide yet muscular middle-aged woman with dark-brown hair wrapped in a bun. She is pleasant but not chatty. "They will be missing their wheeled tub. You may want to take it back now."

"Okay, see you soon."

I take the wheeled tub back just in time to be given another full tub of heavily soiled clothes. This one smells even worse. I'm afraid someone might have died in it. I take it to the soaking tub and start the cycle all over again. Once the soaking tub is full, we stir it for a half an hour and then I take the soaking wet clothes out and wheel them to the white washing machines. A hunchbacked older woman stops me before I get any closer to the white machines.

"Oh, no, you don't. Take those to the black washing machines. The black washing machines are for heavily soiled clothing only." Okay then. I didn't know that.

I wheel my tub to the black washing machines. This worker looks much younger and nicer. In fact, I know her. Dahlia, the deaf girl from my dorm, and another random person put the clothes from my bin into the washing machine. They put soap in the machine and start it. For that I am thankful.

I sign, *this is a tough job* to Dahlia. She's surprised yet thrilled to see me signing. She signs back, *I remember you. I didn't know you could sign! Eat your victuals with me in the break room.* I sign back, *Okay, I will.* I rush off to go get another bin of heavily soiled laundry. I marvel at how mind-numbing this work is. I've lost track of how many tubs of clothes I've moved.

I am starving. It has to be time for 12:00 victuals by now. So, I ask Rebecca. Apparently, the laundry room workers don't get to eat until 1:00. I have another hour. My stomach roars its fury at being underfed at morning victuals, and now having to wait an extra hour for noon victuals.

When a loud shrieky alarm goes off, just like the one in the glass dorm, I throw my gloves away and rush to the black washing machines. A digital clock with red numbers is blinking 1:00 near the washing machines. That is helpful for Dahlia, I'm sure. Dahlia smiles when she sees me and signs, *Follow me.* I force myself to take slower steps than my stomach wants me to take, as I follow Dahlia to the break room.

The much-anticipated break room is surprisingly small for over 100 people. It's gray and bleak. Blah. These poor people. Dahlia and I sit in a back corner because she signs to me that they serve the back first. The tables are smaller, grayer, and more worn out than the tables in the glass dorm. So this is what half the reds I know have to look forward to for the rest of their lives. Several workers in purple jumpsuits bring tall push carts full of victual trays. I can smell hot chicken and gravy—mmm, one of my favorites. I watch the trays being passed out. There are only 12 pink trays for over 100 laundry workers. Huh, I wonder if reds are less boy-crazy than the rest of us in general. That reminds me. Avra had to eat her pink tray today. Ahh, I forgot about her. Oh well. There's nothing I can do about it now. Dahlia gets her tray, but I don't get mine. You have got to be kidding me. I wait until everyone has their tray before I get up and tap one of the purple-clothed workers on the shoulder.

"Excuse me, I didn't get a tray. I am only here for today as a punishment, so I think someone forgot to send my tray down here."

The purple-clad worker says, "Mentor Roberta gave strict instructions that missing a meal is part of your punishment. Sorry." She turns around and leaves the room.

My heart sinks. I realize that this is the first time I've been uncomfortably hungry in my entire life. I wonder how the poor people on the outside do it. *Growl.* My stomach might start to eat itself. I return dejectedly to the table with Dahlia. She may be deaf, but she sure can read faces. As I plop down in my chair, Dahlia hands me her apple with a smile. I take it gratefully and take a bite. I sign, *thank you* to her. The woman with graying black hair sitting next to Dahlia works with her in the washing machine area. She watches me gobble down my apple to the tiniest amount of seeds and strings. Dahlia nudges her. she rolls her eyes and hands over her buttered roll with a hand that has only tiny nubs for fingers.

I smile at her. "Thank you so much. What's your name?"

The woman eyes me unenthusiastically. "Francine, and don't worry about it."

I don't want to waste my time while I'm sitting here. "Tell me, Francine, do you ever get to wear different clothes than jumpsuits?"

"Heh, no."

"Do you get to eat fancy foods like frosted cookies once you have a job here?"

"You mean other than Christmas?"

"Yeah, don't the daily standard meals improve?"

"No way, kid. Enjoy the glass dorm while you've got it. The food and jumpsuits stay the same once you have a job, but the dorms are stacked three bunks high, and they don't change except to add more people. No more glass wall to peek at the boys through, no more classes. Luckily, your job will probably tire you out so much that you'll spend most of your free time sleeping."

That doesn't sound like something to look forward to. Now that I think about it, all the clothing that I've seen come through the laundry chutes are jumpsuits, underwear, and socks. Hmm.

The shriek noise goes off again. I guess it's time to get back to work. I thank Dahlia and Francine for the victuals before I head back to the heavily soiled tub. I watch all the workers around me mindlessly doing their jobs. I can't help but wonder, do they get any satisfaction from their existence? Would I, if I stayed? I stir the heavily soiled jumpsuits around the tub with my paddle, occasionally smiling at one of the unsmiling faces that passes me. I wish I could break these people out. I see Dahlia signing at me across the room, *Less than three hours left. You can do this.* I sign back. *Yes, I can do this.*

I notice after a while that the garbage tub is getting full. I ask the dirty sorter, "Can I take that out for you?"

She says, "You can, but you'll have to get some help with it once you get to the other side of the laundry room."

"Okay. No problem." I grab the garbage tub and immediately realize that this is way less stinky than the heavily soiled laundry. I should have volunteered for this job at the beginning of the day. There is one jumpsuit covered in blood, but it is wrapped in a transparent plastic sack, so I can't smell it. It takes me about three minutes to get across the laundry facility.

I ask a girl with bushy blonde hair and a missing eye in the folding room, "What should I do with the garbage now?" She rolls her eye at me as she comes out of the folding room.

"You must be new here." She pulls a plastic helmet with a plastic dress connected to it off a hook on the wall and onto her body. She puts on a pair of elbow-length gloves that she pulls from a box on the wall. She mumbles and points from her protective suit that I need to put on the other suit that is hanging on the wall. I slip it on. Ugh. This is almost as bad as those horrible guard suits. This helmet is sucking the air out of me. I'm definitely claustrophobic. The bushy blonde walks over to a trap door on the wall. It looks like the trap door for the laundry chute in the glass dorm, except bigger, and it has a locking mechanism. It's big enough that I could probably climb inside... The girl twists the mechanism to open the chute door with a grunt. It creaks and groans as she opens it up. She takes a deep breath then starts throwing garbage bags into the hole. I realize as I stick the plastic bag with the bloody jumpsuit out the chute that I see a glimpse of daylight! There is only a flimsy black plastic flap separating me from the outside of the complex.

As I stick the next bag of garbage through the hole, I reach my arm through the flap and wave it around. I can't wait to tell Avra that my arm has been outside! I am almost too excited to ask, "Where does all the garbage go?"

I can barely hear the blonde through her muffled suit. "There is a garbage truck parked on the outside of this wall. The garbage falls into the truck, and when it is full, the garbage truck takes it to a landfill."

"But we're in the basement. How can there be a truck below us?"

"I asked the supervisor the same thing when I first started working here. This isn't a deep basement, and they've dug out and paved a ramp for the truck to back in and out of. It's a convenience thing."

"Interesting, they get someone to risk the toxins to drive the garbage off."

"I'm sure they wear guard suits that are better than these things. I don't think they care if I suck in a few extra toxins." We finish throwing out the garbage, close the chute, and hang our suits on their hooks.

I look at the unhappy blonde who's trying to catch

her breath next to me. "You aren't treated like you're worth anything in your dorm or your work, are you?"

"Not really."

My heart goes out to her; she has no idea that she's being used and lied to. "I'm not either. I'm actually being punished for doing something that wasn't a big deal." I look around the gray laundry room. This place is the pits. I'm glad I don't have to come back tomorrow. "Say, when does your shift end?"

"When the evening victuals are ready, about 6:00."

"Yuck, that's an hour later than I usually eat. Does anyone come back here after that?"

"No. The laundry builds up all night, but we don't start on it until 8:00 the next morning."

My blood starts pumping faster. "So, no one is in the laundry room from 6:00 pm till 8:00 am, is that right?"

"Yep. Don't be all judgy about that. Nine hours of laundry a day is enough. I don't want my shift to be any longer than it already is, so don't go blabbing to a mentor or a facilitator about it." The blonde girl pokes me in the chest rather forcefully to emphasize her point.

I rub the spot. "Oh, I won't. What's your name by the way?"

She eyes me warily. "Cybil. Why? Do you want to make up a song about Cybil the Cyclops?"

"No! I would never. Look at me, I have an ugly eye too."

179

Cybil looks at my raccoon eye and nods. "I'll see you around, Cybil." She grunts at me and walks back to the folding room.

I almost skip back to the chute room. This has been a successful day's work.

Chapter 21

I AM EXHAUSTED and once again starving as I plop into bed early. My back hurts, my feet hurt, my arms hurt. I thought the laundry room was for wimps. Boy was I wrong.

Avra is in a better mood tonight. She sits on the edge of her bed and looks at me with sympathy. "I missed you in class today."

I smile half-heartedly at her. "Huh, I thought I was just a crazy person."

"You are a crazy person, but you're my crazy person."

A real smile spreads across my face. Yay! We're friends

again. "I learned the ways of the laundry room. It was very educational."

"I'm sure it was. Your boy gang seemed distraught not to see you today."

"Really? I'm surprised you noticed that. You are so anti-boy lately."

Avra picks lost hairs off her pillow. "I ate your tray for 12:00 and 5:00 victuals today. Mentor Maxine knew what I was doing and didn't seem to mind."

My hunger pains start to scream out from the inside. I roll on my side and hug my stomach tightly. "I-I'm glad someone enjoyed them." *Growl.* I didn't get out of the laundry room until 6:00 and all the trays in the glass room were gone by then. I can't believe I didn't get a single full-sized meal today. If I wasn't trying to plan a break-out, I would complain.

"I think you're right about the pink trays, Elira. I wrote back and forth with Scott during exploration time today, and he told me how different I've been. I feel better today than I have in a while. I feel awake."

"Good. Don't eat the pink trays again."

Avra climbs into her bed and pulls the covers up to her chin. "How will I hide the medicated food I don't eat from Mentor Roberta?"

"We'll figure it out. We may have to wrap it in napkins and put it in our pockets till we can flush it down the toilet."

"Huh, you have a plan for everything."

Tell that to my stomach. "Yeah, I do."

I hear Avra start to snore softly. I'm glad she can sleep. I'm not so sure my sleep will be restful. My stomach won't quit growling, and I have at least a million and one things on my mind right now. I hear someone open the door to our room and walk toward me. I'm too tired to turn around and see who it is.

"Are you okay, Elira?" Mentor Maxine asks. She sets a roll on my pillow.

Oh good, I'm glad it's her. I sit up and dig thankfully into the roll. "Yes. I'm fine. I'm just tired and feel like the world is counting on me to save it."

"I'm sure you do, you poor thing. Did you learn anything helpful in the laundry room?"

I whisper excitedly, "Yes. I know how to get out."

Maxine looks around and lowers her voice. "Good. Remember that your pink trays start in six days. You should leave before then if you can. I've been shielding you from the complex's plans for you, but I can't do much more without being exposed."

I listen to the silence of the room for a minute. "Maxine, why does the complex lie to us? It's almost impossible to escape. Why bother teaching us, feeding us in organized trays? I think it would save time and resources to just throw us all together, different ages, different sexes, and make us work."

"Actually, years ago, when the complex system first started, that is what they did. Every child was sterilized and thrown together. No mentors, no school, no structure, but then it was obvious that there was also no work being done."

I remember the pamphlet on babies and cringe at the thought of sterilization. Maxine continues, "The damaged, as you were called, were angry and spent their days fighting each other and the few employees that ran the complex. That's when the boys were separated from the girls. Both groups still weren't very productive workers. So, they started separating and lying to the new kids coming in. They made them feel grateful for the safety they had from the presumably toxic world. They were thankful that their parents supposedly loved them so much to pay for an expensive place in this glorious facility. A grateful heart is a happy and productive heart."

Maxine smiles humorlessly and shakes her head. "Changing to a bigger, better dorm each year gave you all something to look forward to. Schooling made you all smarter and more careful around the machinery. The glass wall lets us know who will be too distracted to work with the opposite sex or needs to be medicated to do so. This complex supplies millions of goods for the hearty outside the complex for a very low cost. Obviously, you don't get paid to work, so the world gets goods that are tedious to make for cheap, and your unfavorable deformities don't get seen or passed on."

Wow, I am learning so much today. "What is the point

of the yellow, orange, and red buttons? To make us judge each other?"

"The real reason is so we mentors don't expect anything that is not reasonable from you. Yellows can do any job. Oranges can only do jobs that they have all the necessary body function for, and reds we have to pick jobs very carefully for or they will exhaust themselves and be unprofitable. You residents, as I call you, seem to use the buttons to classify each other. It is mean and hurtful, but it also gives you something to focus on instead of figuring out how to escape."

"I see why I'm on the watch list now."

Maxine chuckles quietly. "You've never been like everyone else. These thoughts and skills you have will help you survive out there, Elira. Be proud of yourself. If you are successful, you will be the first person to successfully escape in the last 40 years."

"That isn't the hard part. I feel responsible for everyone I'm taking with me. What if they can't handle it out there? What if we get caught? What if we starve? I don't want to be responsible for their deaths."

Maxine looks at Avra's sleeping figure. "If you don't leave soon, at least one of them will die anyway." She looks out the guard-less window. "Luckily, you have at least one friend on the outside."

I imagine Rocky's mom sticking her head out of the bush, "I don't want to see her, Maxine. I don't know how to get her son Rocky out of his cell. I want to give her good news, but I can't."

"So that's Rocky's mom. She is known for her hatred of the complex system on the outside. You will need her help when you get out. Keep communicating with her. I did hear that Rocky is taking the medicated food now. He may be released back to his dorm. I will try to encourage that outcome."

I cover my eyes with my hand. "Even if he is released, he won't be his usual cunning self. It'll be a pain to get him to escape if he's anything like Avra on medicine. I'm sure his mom will be thrilled to see her son as a zombie."

"The medicine wears off—that's why it is mixed into every meal. She will be thrilled to see him. I'll leave you now, so you can sign with her. By the way, the school rooms are being painted tomorrow. The light switch plates and vent covers will be taken off after 5:00 victuals and not put on again until the paint is dry the next morning..."

Oh! That is timely news. "Thank you, Mentor Maxine." I couldn't have gotten this far without her. She leaves and I start plotting my escape plan on one of my pilfered pieces of paper. I must get us out before my pink trays start. I don't know how I can keep Avra and myself nourished and sharp enough to escape otherwise. I kneel on the end of my bed and look out the window. The guard is leaning against the wall facing the other direction. I'm pretty sure he's asleep. I see the mysterious woman peeking through the trees. I sign, *I am Elira. What is your name?*

She signs back, *I am Ernestine. How is Rocky?*

He's in trouble. We are going to escape in five days. Can you help us?

Yes. I will help. What kind of trouble is Rocky in?

He is being medicated so he won't feel anything. Do you know where the garbage chute is?

Yes.

We will escape through the garbage chute at about 12:00 midnight in five days. Help us.

Vanessa starts screaming in her sleep. I sign, *I have to go. Bye.* I walk over to Vanessa's bed and shake her until she wakes up. She is confused and scared. I calm her down and tuck her back in. I go back to my bed and hope that my stomach will quit growling, so I can sleep.

Chapter 22

I'VE NEVER BEEN SO GRATEFUL for my morning victuals before. I only eat half my eggs, bacon, and hash browns, but my stomach stops trying to eat itself. I almost tell Avra to eat her own pink tray so I can have all my victuals. But, she's trusting me, so I better keep my word about sharing my food. I don't know if Shasta is feeling sorry for me, or if she really doesn't like hash browns, but she gives me hers. Shasta is one of those people you want in your corner, or at your table. She hasn't told on me for rigging the pink tray system. I wonder if I can count on her help later...

The twins' faces are framed in the glass wall as I walk into the school room. The expressions on their faces go from worry and concern to excitement and relief in the blink of an eye. A smile creeps onto my face. Their reaction gives me a boost that I didn't know I needed. I hope I can keep myself calm until exploration time. Avra bounces over to me and announces that I'm third on the telephone list. Good. I can tell one of my gang to meet me tonight at the grate. We can work through the details of my plan then. The only thing is I signed up to talk to Rocky a couple of days ago... If he is out of his cell, and medicated, that might be an interesting conversation.

I force my eyes away from the twins and watch the boys' school room door for a minute, hoping that Rocky is okay. A green-clad mentor enters the room with Rocky by his side. He seems... calm and subdued. I miss his contagious smile. I wonder what they put him through.

Mentor Bridget commands us all to turn around because it's time to start class. Avra rolls her eyes at me as we try to switch gears. It is going to be impossible to study today.

Exploration time finally arrives. I turn around and sign to Jefrey that I need to talk to him. He looks at me questioningly. Oh, I guess he hasn't learned sign language like Garth and Rocky. Dang. I grab the scrap paper that Tessa left on her desk and start writing to Jefrey.

It's my turn to use the telephone before I finish my note. Avra pulls me out of my chair and shields me from the other girls as I pick up the telephone and look Rocky straight in the eyes. The medicine is affecting him, but I can still see his intelligent mind looking back at me. I hope the news I'm about to share doesn't send him to a private cell again.

I smile hesitantly at him. "Hi, Rocky. I'm so glad they let you out."

"It's good to be out. I hope you have good news for me."

"Actually, I have two big things to tell you. One is that they are painting the school rooms tonight. I need to talk to the twins about that in a minute." Rocky nods stiffly at me. I take a deep breath. "The other one is rather personal. Do you remember the woman we've seen outside?"

He stares at me emotionlessly. "Yes."

"I know who she is, and why she lingers around the complex every night."

"Who is she? Will she help us escape?"

I'm shocked that he is still on board with the plan. I lower my voice. "Do you still want to escape?"

"Yes, more than anything. These people are cruel. I was right about everything. It's all a lie."

I breathe a sigh of relief. "I thought maybe they had brainwashed you into not wanting to escape."

"Their medicine isn't that good. It just makes girls unappealing to me. I've answered their questions well enough to satisfy them for now." His eyes darken. "I have stories for you that I don't have time to tell right now." Rocky turns around and sees both mentors leaning against the doorframe across the

191

room staring at him. He turns back around. "They are watching me closely. I'll have to keep eating the medicated trays. I'm sorry I won't be much help with the escape. Will the woman help us get away from here? Who is she?"

"I need you to prepare yourself..."

"She knows my mom. Doesn't she?"

"She is your mom, Rocky."

Rocky's eyes are battling back and forth. I think the medicine is telling him not to feel love, yet his inner strength tells him he was right.

Rocky's voice deepens. "I knew it. I knew my parents were alive. She will help us. She wants me back."

"Yes. You were right. I've been communicating with her, and she will help us once we're out. I have a plan. Try not to eat much of the medicated food. I know they are watching you, but try. I need your mind focused."

"I know you do. I'll try. I meant to lead out on this escape, but I blew it. Thank you for taking over. You are exactly the person we need right now."

His praise makes me blush. "We aren't out yet. I'm just trying to save Avra's life and uncover the truth. Rocky, your observations have changed everything for us." I nod at Avra, who's flirting with Scott, and the twins standing guard. I notice Bryon sitting at a desk helping a boy with a misshapen head with his homework. "Should we try to get Bryon on board? He used to be part of this gang."

Garth overhears what I say and leans over the telephone receiver. "I wish we could, but the medicated food has changed him too much. He doesn't believe in the cause anymore. His new life goal is to get everyone to do the extra credit problems."

Pity flows through me as I look at Bryon. "Well, that used to be a good goal. I hate to leave him behind."

Rocky nods. "I do too, but we've tried. He doesn't want to leave."

Jefrey glares at Rocky as he hears that. Rocky looks at Jefrey apologetically. He turns back to me. "We can do this. Do you still want to talk to Jefrey? I can give him some time. He doesn't know sign language."

"Yes. Thank you, Rocky." Rocky hands the telephone to Jefrey and takes a few steps away to give us privacy. Garth, on the other hand, takes a step closer to his brother.

Jefrey hides his annoyance when he gets on and flashes me a stunning smile. "Hey, beautiful. What's up?"

I blush and smile at him; I could look into those eyes all day. Unfortunately, we need to talk business. "They are painting the school rooms tonight after we leave for victuals. Meet me at 10:00 by the cold air return."

Jefrey's head droops. "I don't think they'll let me. The mentors will be guarding the door." The loud, annoying timer goes off.

I hurriedly spout off, "Use your ingenuity. Create a distraction. See you tonight!"

"Uh, I don't know, I'll try." I smile encouragingly at him as bossy Mara flips her white blonde hair at me and gets in my face. "Get off the telephone, Elira. My turn!"

MY MIND IS GOING a million miles a minute the whole time I'm eating my victuals. Avra doesn't say anything, but her eyes say that she is concerned about me. How do I make sure people stay out of the school room while I'm inside? Mentor Maxine and the loud shriek we all despise comes to my rescue. Announcement time.

Everyone gathers in the common room to hear what the announcement is. Maxine clears her throat and says, "The school room walls are being painted as we speak. The complex chief ordered it to be done as soon as possible. The wet paint will ruin clothing and is slightly toxic to breathe in. The workers will be wearing masks. If you value your health, you will stay out of there this evening. You are not allowed to enter that room until the paint is dry and the area has been cleaned up. It will be ready for morning classes tomorrow."

Perfect! I don't care about toxins, but everyone else does. I try not to look overly interested as the workers in white jump suits march into the dorm with ladders and paint cans.

"Elira, are my bald spots noticeable? I don't want Scott to

see them," Avra says as she mournfully runs her fingers through her hair.

Mmm, I don't want to hurt her feelings, but her bald spots are getting worse. "Actually, I have an idea on how to hide them better."

I have Avra sit on the ground in front of me as I sit on a white sofa. I braid her hair. It will hide her bald spots much better than when all of her hair is down. I keep one eye on Avra's head and one eye on the school room door. The workers haven't left the school room by the time I finish the braid. I encourage Avra to practice sign language with me. I know quite a few basic words now. It's so much faster than spelling out each word. Rocky's mom has known my signs so far. I keep checking the school room door to see if they are done painting yet. Nope. They are probably close, but not done yet.

Avra wants to go to bed early, so as she gets ready, I write a letter to Garth detailing my plan. I tell him I'm sorry I couldn't meet with him on inspection day. I tell him to meet me in the school room at 10:00 pm the next day. I'll get to talk to Jefrey tonight, and I'm afraid Rocky is being watched too closely to risk giving him my plans. I feel like I have to keep things fair between the twins.

Almost everyone goes to bed half an hour before the painters leave. I bite all my fingernails off while waiting. Once the painters are done, they haul out all the equipment that they can carry in one trip.

The head painter addresses Maxine as they walk. "Maxine, we'll haul the rest of the equipment out in the morning."

"That's fine. Thank you. Have a good night."

I'm about to tell Mentor Maxine that I'm going in the school room when Mentor Roberta walks through the dormitory door. She approaches us, whispers a few words to Mentor Maxine, then sits down on a white sofa in the common room and starts writing on her clipboard.

Maxine winks at me as she leaves. "I'll see you later, Elira. Get a good night's sleep." Oh no, Mentor Roberta's on the night shift tonight. Now what do I do? I hurriedly leave the room to change into my pajama jumpsuit and brush my teeth.

I hear someone coughing hard in the room with all the sick reds, like from the toenails up style coughing. Hmm. I wait a full three minutes, walk into the common room, and approach Mentor Roberta. Her head jerks up, and she glares at me. "What are you doing up?"

"Someone is coughing really hard in the sick red room by the bathroom. I really can't sleep with all that racket. Is there any medicine that can help her?"

Mentor Roberta taps her fingers on her clipboard. "Yes, there is some strong cough medicine in the doctor's office. I'll have to go get it. You go back to bed, and I'll be right back with the medicine."

"Oh good, thank you, Mentor Roberta." I head back to my room, glancing back to make sure she leaves. I run into my room and stuff all of my clothes and my gray duffel bag under my blankets, so it looks like I'm sleeping with the covers over my head. Avra is sound asleep; I hope everyone else is too. Quietly, I speed walk to the school room, just in the nick of time. Click. Mentor Roberta unlocks the door to the dorm. I hear her walking toward the bedrooms.

I do a happy dance as I walk around the ladders and paint cans to get to the glass wall. I stop dancing as I get to the hole where the grate should be. Jefrey isn't there. No one is. I touch the paint on the wall. It is white like everything else in this dorm, and it is drying fast, it's just a little tacky. Hmm. I sit down in front of the hole. Both grate covers are off. I take the sound barrier out and look straight into the boys' school room. What a waste! Where is Jefrey? I look at the clock propped up against one of the ladders. It says 10:15. Did I miss him already? Are they guarding the door more heavily on his side? I don't dare leave my note for Garth. The workers would find it when they put the vent plates back on in the morning. I stick my hand through the hole and wave it around the boys' school room. I bet no other girl in the complex has ever done this! Just like the garbage chute door though, I won't have the opportunity to tell anyone. I touch the wet, white paint on the boy side with my fingers. Their paint is wetter than ours. My two middle fingers look like white eyeballs on the tips as I look at them. I bet I've left finger prints on their side. Oh well. I'm sure the painters will think they did it, and the grate cover will hide it.

I stand up to leave when I see Jefrey's handsome figure walking across his school room. Hooray! I sit back down and smile through the hole. Jefrey plops down on the other side, but his face doesn't smile back at me, which lessens my excitement.

Jefrey opens his mouth but pauses for several seconds before saying, "I almost got caught sneaking in here, Elira. This is a bad idea. One of the painters asked me what I was doing as he left and I was coming in. I told him I was sleep walking. Somehow, he believed me. I had to go back to my room and wait for 15 minutes before trying again."

I can't help but laugh. "Ha ha! That is funny! I'm glad you came back."

Jefrey's scowl turns into a smile. He reaches through the hole and takes my hand. My fingers tremble as I feel his warm skin against mine. Why does this feel so different from when I touch Avra's hand?

"I'm glad I came back too. Wow. Your hand is so small and soft. It's just like I imagined it would be."

I try hard not to blush and will my hand to stop trembling as he holds it. "I am breaking out of the complex in four days. Will you come with me?"

Jefrey's smile turns back into a scowl. He lets go of my hand and pulls his back into his school room. I put my hand back into my lap dejectedly.

"What if Rocky is wrong and it's toxic outside?"

"He's not wrong. Mentor Maxine told me that this whole

complex life is a lie. They lie to us so we'll happily stay in here, with our undesirable deformities, away from the rest of the world, and make goods for free."

Jefrey shakes his head silently.

"My best friend Avra is too sick for a job, and they are going to kill her. I have to go. Now." I sigh and look at him with pleading eyes. "Will you come with me or not?"

Jefrey looks down at his hands. I see that he has a purplish spot between his middle fingers. He rubs it in a nervous way and then looks at me. His beautiful blue eyes are stormy and agitated.

"I think it's a bad idea. We know nothing about surviving out there. We've never even skipped a meal before."

"Speak for yourself." My stomach growls louder than ever to back me up. "You don't have to come, but Avra, Rocky, and I are leaving in four days through the laundry and garbage chutes. I've been communicating with Rocky's mom, who's outside, through my window. She's going to help us. I want you and Garth to come too."

Jefrey clenches his fists. "I know Garth will go anywhere Rocky and you go. I can't stay here and let you leave with him. I—I'm coming too."

I let out a sigh of relief. "Good. I have written down my plan in full. I've addressed this to Garth, but all of you should read it, then destroy it."

Jefrey recoils. "Why did you write it to Garth?"

"I am here holding your hand through the hole, Jefrey. I was trying to be fair, that's all."

Jefrey reaches through the hole and takes my hand again. This time he kisses it. My hand flinches as his warm, wet lips touch my skin. I am so shocked that I just stop talking and stare at him. We can hear a loud voice say, "Mentor Jim, I have a terrible stomach ache. I can't sleep; will you get me some medicine?"

Jefrey releases my hand. "That's the sign from Garth. Mentor Jim was about to come in here. I have to go. I will come with you Elira. I'll talk to you later and... hold your hand again soon." Jefrey holds up my note in salute and then gets up and leaves the room.

I sit there in shock for a moment. I look at the hand he kissed. It looks the same as it always has, but it feels different. It feels like it's alive for the first time. I smell my hand and then hold it against my cheek. What am I going to do when I'm outside with both twins, able to talk and touch them whenever I want? That thought sends goosebumps up my arms. I put the sound barrier back in, stand up, and walk to the door. How am I going to get out of here? Mentor Roberta is probably back on the sofa. I peek out the door, yep, she is.

Is there anything in here that can help me? I spot a random red button on the ground under the plastic protecting the carpet. I pull it out from under the plastic and peek out the door into the dining area. Mentor Roberta has her back to me. I walk as close as I can to her without being heard and then throw the button at the far-left door that leads to the bedrooms. Mentor Roberta looks up from her clipboard and walks to the left side door and picks up the button lying there. I run through the open right-side door and slip into the right-side bathroom. I press my back to the door and catch my breath. I flush the nearest toilet and turn on the sink. When I open the door, Mentor Roberta is standing face to face with me.

"Did you throw this button at the door, Elira?" she asks as she shows me the red button in her hand.

I rub my eyes like I've just woken up. "Be serious, I don't have any red buttons."

Mentor Roberta is not convinced. "No one else is awake except you."

"I haven't been awake long. I had to go to the bathroom."

"Why didn't you use the bathroom right next to your room?"

I fake a yawn. "Good question... I guess I was sort of sleep walking."

Mentor Roberta gives me a skeptical look. "So where do you think this button came from?"

"I really couldn't say. Shasta is notoriously feisty in her sleep, and she has red buttons. Maybe she chucked it in her sleep."

Mentor Roberta closes her fingers around the button and

squeezes it, making a fist. "Go back to bed, and don't get out again. I don't care what your excuse is."

"Yes, Mentor Roberta," I squeak as I swerve around her and head straight for my room. I throw all my stuff out of my bed onto the floor and climb in. I pull the blanket over my head and try to calm my thumping heart. Man, that couldn't have been any closer.

Chapter 23

I AM LEARNING TO DEAL with my hunger better now. Splitting my victuals with Avra is harder on me than it is on her. She doesn't eat much anyway. Stuffing her medicated food in my pockets, I go to the bathroom to flush the medicated food down the toilet after each meal. I feel like a genius until someone notices.

Mentor Roberta corners me when I come out of the bathroom after morning victuals. "I have noticed that you spend a large amount of time in the bathroom, Elira."

"Uh, yeah. Sorry."

"Especially after meals. You look skinnier to me. Are you

203

throwing up after you eat?" I laugh but quickly turn it into a cough. "That is called bulimia and it can kill you. Being thin is not worth throwing away your health for."

I try to keep a straight face. "No, Mentor Roberta. I hate throwing up; I would never do that on purpose. I just have an upset stomach."

"I've had several people say that lately. I hope the flu isn't being passed around. I will get you some medicine to take with your noon victuals."

"That would be very helpful. Thank you, Mentor Roberta." The things I do to cover my tracks...

My boy gang is looking at me through the glass a lot this morning. I think they've read my plan and are eager and anxious about it. I take the medicine Mentor Roberta gives me at noon victuals. I hope it doesn't upset my empty stomach too much.

When exploration time comes, none of my boys approach the glass. Garth signs to me, *They are watching us; we'll talk tonight.* I try not to let my apprehension get to me.

At evening victuals, Mentor Maxine gives Avra her own normal colored tray. "Josephine is sick and can't eat hers. You two need to get your strength back."

"Thank you, Maxine. You're a lifesaver." I shovel a few bites into my mouth in appreciation. "I need to get into the school room tonight. Will you help me?"

"Yes, I'm doing a double shift tonight. Do what you need to."

"Perfect, thank you."

I eat every bite of my chicken-vegetable soup, roll, and oatmeal cookie like it's my last meal, then slip the squarish spoon into my pocket.

I whisper my plan to Avra. She nods, but isn't feeling well enough to help me. I tell her to lay down and not to worry about me. I need to go to the bathroom before my meeting with Garth, so I go into the closest bathroom and lock myself in a stall. As I do my business, I hear the door open again, and several shuffling feet enter.

"I already told her that she couldn't have four boys all to herself. She said that those boys only like girls who do extra credit problems." Yay. It's Vanessa.

"That's ridiculous. I think she has cast some kind of spell on them. Who in their right mind would like a girl with a big purple blotch across her eye? I don't get it. They won't look at anyone else but her." Great. I'm pretty sure the only person who would say that in this dorm is Julie.

"Rocky has given me some attention before."

"Yeah, but that was before they hauled him off, right?"

"Yeah."

"He's nothing compared to those twins. I would give up my dessert for a month to have one five-minute conversation with the yellow button twin." Ahh! Julie better stay away from Jefrey.

I've had enough. *Flush.* I strut from the stall to the sinks. "Hello, Vanessa, Julie, and Mara. It's nice to see you three having such a positive bonding moment together in the bathroom."

Julie glares at me. "You are the most smug, annoying human being I have ever met. If I could get away with it, I'd slap that smirk off your face right now."

I look in the mirror at myself. "Yeah. I believe you. Unfortunately for you, Mentor Bridget told me that if you do one more thing to anyone, she'll charge you as a dissident." Julie growls like a wild animal, but she doesn't say anything to me.

Mara flips her white-blonde hair at me. "I don't get it. You aren't even pretty. What do those gorgeous twins see in you?"

I take my time drying my hands. I pat Vanessa on the head. "Brains," I say sweetly and shut the door in their faces.

AT TEN O'CLOCK, I make sure Avra and everyone else in my room is asleep before I sneak out of my room and into the common room. I see a mentor-issued flashlight sitting on the edge of a table on the way to the school room. Mentor Maxine is sitting on a white chair with her back to me, reading a book. She does not turn toward me as she says, "They are

trying to keep the cost of electricity down in the complex. We
have to shut off all unnecessary lights from now on."

I grab the flashlight as I slip quietly into the dark school
room. I click the flashlight on as I walk through the door.

The empty classroom is kind of creepy in the dark. I see
someone on the other side of the glass with a flashlight. I feel
my pulse quicken as I walk to the glass wall hoping I'm not
about to face off with a mentor... Nope, it's Garth in all his
handsome glory. Good, this is going to work. I smile at him
as I rush to the corner of the room and unscrew the screws
with the stolen spoon. I try to pop out the sound barrier, but
it's stuck. I focus on the corner that seems stuck when I feel
something warm on my other hand. I look up to see that Garth
has unscrewed his side of the vent cover too. He takes the
sound barrier through his side and then takes my hand in his
deformed one. I am in awe that he would do this. It's so rare to
have someone help me out. His hand is a little bit bigger than
Jefrey's. It's strong and warm. I love it.

"Elira, are you ready to escape with me?" Oh, that voice.

My quivering lips smile. "Y-yes. I have it all worked out,
but you'll have to hide your hand when we're out there." Garth
glances down at his hand with the stuck together fingers, no
self-consciousness showing. I touch my raccoon-eye birthmark.
"I'll have to stay indoors all the time. I obviously can't hide my
face very well."

He reaches his empty hand toward me and pushes my hair

behind my birthmark-framed ear so he can see the purplish line better. He takes his thumb and gently traces my scar from my eyelid back to my ear. It is such a gentle and intimate gesture; I feel myself melting into a puddle. I want to climb through the vent hole and wrap my arms around him. But that is inappropriate. I need to keep my unmedicated emotions in check.

I clear my throat. "Is Jefrey going to come with us? He seems unsure about it."

"Yes. He says he is. I'm glad. I would hate to leave my brother behind."

"I hope I don't have to leave Avra behind. She says she'll go, but she is weak, and I don't know if she can survive on less-than-ideal food and shelter."

Garth looks into my eyes and voices what I'm not revealing. "Would she rather die free with us or die here in a few weeks when the death doctor is told to finish her off?"

His words fill me with emotion. "I'm sure she'd rather die free, but she thinks I'm crazy."

Garth rubs my hand with his less-than-perfect fingers. "You're not crazy. You are smart, brave, and beautiful. I wish I could leave with you right now."

I smile and blush at his compliment. "I wish we could too. It won't be long. Three days will be here before we know it."

Garth gives my hand a squeeze as he starts talking business. "I've been thinking about the logistics of what we're doing. We should wear three jumpsuits each when we leave. Who knows how we'll get clothing out there." Wow, he is so different from his brother.

"This kind of clothing may give us away though. Rocky's mom doesn't wear these. I'll ask her to find us some clothes like hers if she can, plus, food and everything else we'll need. Is that too much to ask of a complete stranger?"

Garth laughs. "Ha! Usually yes, but since she's Rocky's mom, I'm going to guess, no."

"I hope you're right."

Garth looks at my fingers, memorizing every detail. "I'm so excited to leave this place with you."

My cheeks grow warm and my heart speeds up. "You probably won't feel the same way when you see the beautiful girls with no deformities on the outside, Garth."

"No, I won't. You'll see. I only have eyes for you."

I worry that the blush on my cheeks will become permanent. "Speaking of eyes, your eyes are my favorite thing about you. They are so breathtakingly blue. I feel like I could fall into them and never come back."

Garth tilts his head to the side. "Do you feel the same way about Jefrey's eyes?"

It feels like ice cold water hits me in the face with that remark. "I—I am so sorry, Garth, but I like you both. I'm sure when we're on the outside, everyone's feelings will become clearer."

Garth nods his head. "I knew this day would come. I really didn't want my brother and I to fall for the same girl, or have the same girl fall for both of us. We look the same, but we are very different people."

I feel my heart racing. "I know. Please don't make me decide right now. I'm just barely getting to know you both."

Garth looks at me with compassion mixed with a touch of jealousy. "You're right. I won't make you decide any time soon. Just know, that I knew you were special. I told Rocky that we should write to you that first day. I think of you as a beautiful angel and our liberator. I believe in your plan, and I'll help you in any way I can."

"Uh, I-I just know how the laundry system works. I'm not special. If you want to help me, gather as much food as you can and anything else that will help us on the outside."

"Okay, I will."

"Thank you."

"I would do anything for you."

"Ha ha, I'll keep that in mind. We should go. I need to sign with Rocky's mom still tonight."

The light in Garth's eyes dims a bit. "But I don't want to say goodbye."

Aw. If only we didn't have to. "I know what you mean, but we'll see each other soon." I try to memorize his face just like this in the few seconds I have left. "Goodbye, Garth."

"I love hearing your voice say my name. Goodbye, Elira."

I am frozen to my spot as I watch Garth put the sound barrier back in the cold air return. He keeps his eyes on me as he works. I'm amazed at how easily he uses his hand with the fingers stuck together. He smiles at me one last time before he puts his grate cover back on. Now that I can't see him, my body unfreezes. I take a deep breath and let it out as I screw my metal cover back on. He's already standing with his flashlight and watches me stand up. I see his mouth form the words *good night*. The silence of the thick glass wall is loud to my hungry ears. I force a smile and mouth *good night* back. I force my feet to move away from the glass wall. I can't let myself turn around again at the door or I won't leave.

I walk out the door, then wonder if it's been Garth or Jefrey who looks back at me before leaving the school room most days. I pop my head back in the classroom expectantly. Whether it's Garth or not, I don't know, because it's dark, and he is already gone.

Mentor Maxine's eyes move from her book to me, to her book again. I smile and give her a thumbs-up sign. She smiles and nods but doesn't look at me as I walk to my room.

The guard must not be watching me anymore. He isn't in front of my window yet again. Ernestine is peeking through the trees when I look out the window. I wave to her and sign, *I have five people escaping in three days. Two girls and three boys. Can you get us clothes?*

Ernestine signs back, *Yes, if Rocky is one of them.*

211

I nod. *He is. Will you help us get out of the garbage truck?*

Her fingers move quickly. *Yes. The garbage chute is a good idea. I will be ready to get you out of there. If I'm not by the truck, I'll be hiding from the guards behind the tree line.*

Will people notice my birthmark? I trace my raccoon eye with my finger, just in case she can't see it properly from so far away.

Yes. You will have to hide your face always.

I was afraid she would say that. I guess I have lived hidden my whole life anyway. I shouldn't be sad that I will continue to do that on the outside. *How cold is it out there?*

It is March. It is a bit cold, but it's not freezing anymore. I will take you to my house and feed you. Do not worry. I will take care of you.

Thank you, Ernestine. I must sleep now.

I've been waiting many years for this. Thank you for giving me my son, Elira. Ernestine's eyes tear up with emotion. I wonder how many years she has been waiting for this to happen. What a devoted mother.

Chapter 24

I SHOULD HAVE SEEN THIS COMING, but I've had too many things on my mind lately. Avra is not happy with me. She just realized that I have not included Scott in our escape plans. She insists that Scott has to come with us. I tell her that I haven't asked Ernestine to accommodate six people and I can't keep abusing her generosity.

Avra stomps her foot as we make our beds. "If Scott can't go, then I won't go."

I slam my sock drawer shut and whisper loudly, "Avra, if you don't go, you will die."

Avra's eyes fill with tears. "I'd rather die than live without him."

Give me a break. I consider making her eat her own pink trays until we leave… That would stop this Scott obsession. But will she be useless to me during a time-sensitive escape? Or, more importantly, would I want her to do the same thing to me if our roles were reversed? Dang.

I sigh. "Okay. I will talk to Ernestine about adding Scott and the gang about getting Scott on board. But he might say no and turn us all in. This could be bad."

"He loves me. I know he'll come. Thank you, Elira!"

"You're welcome." Ahh. I only have today and tomorrow left!

I can't concentrate during morning classes again. Mentor Bridget hands back my assignment. I've missed four questions. She seems confused. "Are you feeling all right, Elira? You rarely miss even one question."

I smile at her as beads of sweat start forming on my forehead. "I feel a little off. But I'm okay. I'll focus harder."

"Okay… If you need to see the doctor, just say the word."

"I'll be all right." I turn around and see Rocky looking at me. I sign, *See if Scott will escape with us. Avra refuses to leave him.* He nods very slowly and imperceptibly at me. Garth and Jefrey lean over to Rocky, and he fills them in on what has to be done. I lay my head on my arm and map out on a piece of scrap paper what is left to be done before we can leave.

My victuals don't feed both Avra and me very well anymore. I can hear not just my stomach growling, but my whole body growling. Shasta gives me her apple, bless her kind soul. When exploration time comes around, I have a cryptic note written about what we are going to do. I hope Scott has an answer for me.

As I approach the glass with Avra, Scott reaches out and presses his hand to the glass. Avra presses hers on top of his. I roll my eyes and check to make sure their mentor has his back turned. I press my note to the glass. Scott reads it as my gang surrounds him to hide my note from anyone else. Scott writes on a piece of paper, *Rocky has talked to me already. Yes, I will come with you.* Avra squeals with delight and bounces up and down. Good, I'm glad that part is going to work out. I just need to get Ernestine on board tonight.

Garth looks at me with concern and signs, *Are you all right?*

I smile at him and sign back, *Yes, I'm just a little stressed.*

Rocky signs, *It will all work out. We are prepared. We have checked out the laundry chute. We will all fit, barely. We won't all be able to wear extra suits though, and we have some fruit and rolls stashed.* Jefrey glares at us. He's annoyed that he's being left out of the conversation. I wish he would have taken the time to learn sign language.

I sign back to Rocky, *Do you have someone in mind who can keep your mentor busy at midnight tomorrow?*

Bryon.

Is he up to it?

Yes, I'm sure he'll keep his promise.

Excellent.

The loud shriek alarm goes off. Jefrey puts his hand on the glass like Scott did, and I see Garth tense up. I hesitantly put my hand on top of Jefrey's. Garth walks away quickly with his hands balled up into fists. I swiftly take my hand off the glass and wave as I walk away.

Avra catches up to me. "You are going to tear those brothers apart, Elira."

I smack myself on the forehead with my palm. "I know."

"You are going to break one of their hearts, especially when we're on the outside not separated by glass. Which one will it be?"

A groan escapes my lips. "I just don't know yet. I'm hoping I'll understand them better on the outside and the answer will become clear."

"And if it doesn't become clear?"

"I-I will make a choice before they kill each other."

"That's right."

At bedtime, I take my time in the bathroom throwing my dirty jumpsuit into the laundry chute. No one else is looking, so I stick one leg in the trap door, then the other. I slide my body down a few inches, then I see if my hips will fit through. They will. I pull myself up again. Hooray, I will fit. Avra is a little bit smaller than me, so I'm sure that she will fit too.

When everyone is asleep in my dorm, I kneel at the end of my bed and look out the window. The glass is cold against my forehead. I don't see Ernestine at first; the guard is walking back and forth along the edge of the building. When he has his back turned and is slowly walking away, Ernestine's head pops through the trees.

My hands move super-fast, so I can finish my sentence before the guard turns around. *One more boy is coming with us. Is that okay?*

Yes. That is fine. I have a generous friend with lots of food and clothes.

Can we trust your friend?

Yes. She is... Ernestine's head and hands disappear as the guard turns around and heads toward my window. I crawl into bed and pull my covers up to my chin. The guard stops in front of my window and looks in at me. What on earth is he doing? This is a girl bedroom, the sicko. He slowly turns around and rests his back against the window. I guess I'm done communicating with Ernestine for the night. That's okay. I need my rest. Tomorrow is going to be a very long and exciting day.

I close my eyes as I hear Avra's voice whisper, "Elira, did she say Scott could come?"

I smile in the dark. "Yes. She said Scott could come."

"Oh good. I need him."

"You will have him. Good night, Avra."

"Good night, Elira."

"Hey, raccoon eye, could you please shut up? Some of us are trying to sleep around here."

I roll my eyes in the dark and yell, "Got it."

Vanessa is such a sweetheart, let me tell you. I won't miss sharing a room with her at all. *Gulp.* Tomorrow night my roommates will be—boys. I wonder if there are some kind of rules about being too close to each other on the outside. If I have to sleep close enough to hear or smell either of the twins, I may never sleep again... I hear footsteps, and I close my eyes before they can see that I'm awake.

"Elira, are you asleep?"

Sigh. "No, Maxine. Are you working tomorrow night?"

"No. Scoot over so I can sit down."

I make room for her. "Dang, we're going to leave then. It would be so much easier if you were on the night shift."

"I will ask Roberta if she will switch me shifts. I can say I have a date or something."

"That would be very helpful." After a few seconds of silence, I ask, "What is a date?"

Maxine flexes each foot and rubs her calves. "Um, it's when a boy and a girl do an activity together to get to know each other better."

I smile at the thought. "Do you do that often?"

"No. Not very often. I'm too busy worrying about you girls."

The smile melts off my face. "I won't be your problem for much longer."

"I'll always care about you. Are you going to stay in my apartment?"

"No. We are staying with Rocky's mom, Ernestine. I think it'll be harder to find us if we're with her instead of you."

"You're probably right. I will check on you after the chaos dies down. There will be an investigation once you escape."

I sit up tall. "Will you get in trouble?"

"Maybe. Like I said before, they could fire me. But they won't hurt me. It's worth getting you guys out, either way."

My eyes fill with tears that I try to keep from spilling over. "Thank you, Maxine. You've always been a good mentor to me. I've learned so much from you. I imagine sometimes that my mother was like you. I will miss you so much."

"I'll miss you too. You are like the child I never had. I'm so proud of you; you will soon be free, and you will save Avra's life."

I feel a tear trickle down my face. I realize that my plan will save some and cause others trouble.

"Good night, Elira."

"Good night, Maxine. Thank you."

Chapter 25

MY EYES POP OPEN as I hear girls moving around and talking. This is it. I am leaving this place with five other people today. I won't sleep in this bed or under this roof ever again. I hope Ernestine is ready to take us on. Six teenagers take a lot of food and space and...

I can't let my anxiety talk me out of this. I get up and walk straight for the showers. Who knows when my next one will be. I stop halfway there, turn around, and head back to my bed. I take all the notes and papers from under my mattress to flush down the toilet. It's time to tie up loose ends. It breaks my heart to flush Garth and Jefrey's notes, but I hope there will be more in the future. The hot water of the shower relaxes my muscles and calms my mind. When I get out and look in the foggy mirror, all I can see in my reflection is fear in my eyes and a bright purplish birthmark that I can't hide. Why do I think I can pull this off?

"You look like you're about to take a big test, Elira. But you're not, so cover up your hideous eye and get out of my spot." Mara says as she brushes her long white hair, smacking me with her brush every so often.

"Good morning to you too," I mumble as I leave the bathroom. There are things I won't miss about this place.

Avra looks at me with apprehension as she makes her bed. "Are we ready for this, Elira?"

I am the leader of this operation. I have to be strong, or at least pretend to be strong for Avra's sake. "Yes. We are ready. Just act normal and say any goodbyes that you need to without being obvious that you are up to something."

"Okay. Let's go eat."

We have bacon, eggs, and toast for morning victuals, and they are so good. Are the victuals on the outside this good, I wonder? Morning classes are pretty boring. I try to appear attentive so Mentor Bridget doesn't get suspicious. I only miss one question on my quiz, so I'm faking it pretty good so far. I sneak a peek at my gang as I leave for 12:00 victuals. Jefrey looks positively sick. His face is white, and he has dark circles under his eyes. Scott seems a little twitchy, but Rocky and Garth look determined. They put their arms around Jefrey and Scott and smile at me. I can't believe it. This is going to work.

Avra is super sweet and complimentary to everyone while we eat. She tells Shasta that she is pretty and kind, and that she has always appreciated her generosity. She even tells Vanessa that she appreciates her diligence in looking out for everyone's safety and health. Avra is such a gem. I should be doing all of this too, but I have no words. All my mental energy is going into the escape. I smile at least. When all these girls reflect on what they know about me tomorrow during the investigation, they'll remember that I smiled and tried to be nice even if I was a little odd.

As I walk back to the school room, I see Mentor Roberta walk in. "Where is Mentor Maxine? I thought she was working this shift."

"No, this is my shift. She wanted to trade, but that was not going to work for me."

"Oh…" I try not to look crestfallen as I walk into the school room, but dang. The escape just got a whole lot harder.

At exploration time, I sign to Garth that Mentor Roberta is going to be on duty tonight, so I need to come up with a diversion.

He signs back, *Bryon is going to pretend to sleep walk into the common room and then curl up on the sofa to fake sleep. Mentor Briggs will shake him and try to wake him up. He's going to fake it long enough to give us time to get down the chute. He'll eventually*

223

wake up and take a long time apologizing for disturbing Mentor Briggs.

Mentor Briggs is on duty tonight?

Yes.

Why are all the hard-nose mentors on duty the night we escape? Dang.

It'll be okay. We can do this.

I don't have any girls that would do that for me. Shasta might do something, but I don't think she'll act like a sleep walker.

You're smart. You'll figure it out.

Why does everyone keep saying that? I am not as competent as they think I am. I sign, *I will figure it out. Make sure all four of you go down the laundry chute at midnight with three jumpsuits on, if it doesn't bulk you up too much, and all the food you've stashed. Get out of the giant hamper quickly or we'll all fall on each other's heads.*

You remember where the garbage chute is from there, right?

Yes.

The garbage truck will be stinky and gross, but Rocky's mom will help us get out quickly. That's going to be the trick. We have to do everything quickly.

Got it.

The loud shriek noise goes off. Covering my ears with my hands, I'm thankful that this is the last time I'll have to hear it. I wave at the gang before I leave the school room. I wish my hands would stop trembling.

At 5:00 victuals, Julie's friend throws up all over their table. The flu really is going around. Mentor Roberta sets her communication box on the table next to me. I could try to break it... Nah, I don't want to cause a scene. Mentor Roberta grabs a garbage bag, and wipes everything from the table into the bag, then sanitizes the table. She puts her arm around Julie's friend and starts walking her to the bedrooms. "Julie, throw that bag into the garbage chute please."

Julie flicks her short dark hair back as she picks up the bag. She doesn't tie a knot around the top and calls out to the room at large, "I'm going to give those laundry workers a fun surprise in the morning." She proceeds to walk to the bathroom with the laundry chute in it.

I look up from staring at Mentor Roberta's communication box. "No, Julie! Don't do that!" I jump out of my seat and try to stop her.

"You can't make me!" Julie runs to the laundry chute and dumps the bag into it.

I shove her in the shoulder. "What kind of sick person are you?"

Julie shoves me back. "Why do you care so much? It's just a prank on people you don't know."

I can't give anything away right now. "I had to help in the laundry one day as a punishment, remember? They are really nice people down there."

"They'll get over it," Julie says as she walks away.

Yeah, but I won't. I open the laundry chute and look down the hole, I wrinkle my nose at the stench of barf. Seriously, can I get any more bad luck today? I mope back into the common room. The distraught look on my face must be obvious, because Shasta comes over. "You seem upset. Can I help?"

"Actually... you can. Are we friends, Shasta?"

"Yes."

I put my arm through hers, walk her into our bedroom, and shut the door so no one can hear us. "If I broke the rules, or did something that was wrong, or dangerous, would you still be my friend?"

Shasta pauses then looks into my eyes. "Yes."

"Would you tell on me?"

"Only if it was a life-or-death bad decision."

I twist my hands together nervously. "What if it was a leave-and-never-come-back decision?"

Shasta appears to be in shock. She lowers her already quiet voice. "You're going to escape the complex?"

"Yes. Tonight."

Shasta scrunches her eyebrows together. "That's crazy. Why would you do that? It's toxic out there."

"I don't have time to tell you all the lies that we've been told, but I heard the complex chief say that if Avra didn't get better, she would be sent to the final doctor, and she wouldn't come back. I can't let that happen."

Shasta's protective side surfaces. "I still think that's crazy, but I understand why you're doing it. I won't tell."

"Will you help me? I would help you."

Shasta looks at her long, skinny fingers for a long time. "Yes. I will help you."

"Avra and I are going down the laundry chute at midnight. I know a way out from there, and we are not coming back. I need someone to distract Mentor Roberta from about 11:50 until 12:30. You would need to keep her in the common room. Tell her you can't sleep, and you want some advice about something."

"I could tell her that I like a boy and I can't stop dreaming about him."

"No! Don't say anything about boys, ever. They will put you on pink medicated trays to stop you from liking boys if you do. Don't do it."

"O-kay. What do I talk to her about then?"

"Say you're being bullied by Julie and you can't sleep because you're having nightmares about her. Tell her every mean thing you've ever seen Julie do. That should keep her preoccupied; she'll be writing things on her clipboard for a while."

"That isn't too far from the truth, really. I can do that."

"Thank you, Shasta. You are a lifesaver. I will never forget you. Trust Mentor Maxine, but don't trust anyone else in this complex. This whole system is built on lies."

Shasta looks at me skeptically. "That is hard to believe, but I do notice things that don't make sense sometimes, like the fancy cookies. If you figure out a way to come back for me, will you?"

"Yes—In fact, move to my bed after we leave. If I figure out a way to break you out, I'll come to that window to communicate with you—at night. Learn sign language from Mentor Bridget after the chaos dies down. I will try my best to come back for you." Shasta wraps her skinny arms around me, and I hug her back.

Chapter 26

I LAY ON MY BED with my covers up to my chin watching the digital clock on the side wall. The red colon keeps blinking. It reminds me of a heartbeat. My heartbeat. I would really like it if my heart was still beating in a few hours. This is a dangerous business I'm in. Two more minutes and then Shasta will get up and go distract Mentor Roberta. I look over at Avra. She is awake and staring at the clock too. Her bottom lip is trembling and so is the rest of her. We have three jumpsuits on under our pajama suits.

I don't think anyone noticed how thick we looked as we slipped into bed last night. Shasta did a good job distracting the room full of girls as we came in from the bathroom by telling a story about how the doctor accidentally switched her medicine with someone else's. Now everyone is asleep, except for the three of us.

11:49. 11:49. 11:49. 11:50. Shasta gets up and whispers to me, "Here goes nothing. Good luck, Elira."

"Thank you, Shasta. For everything."

She walks out of the room. I jump up and stuff my remaining belongings under my covers. They kind of look like a person sleeping. I look at Avra. Her eyes are closed, and a tear is streaming down her face. I take her hand and help her up. "You can do this, Avra. Scott is counting on you."

"I know. Let's go."

We shove her belongings under her blankets as well. Two sleeping dissidents, no one will be any the wiser until morning.

We quietly slip out of our room and down the hall to the right-side bathroom with the laundry chute. Oh great. I see light peeking out from under the door. Someone is using it! It's probably one of the fragile reds. I hear a toilet flush. I whisk Avra into the room full of orange-button girls. I hope they are all asleep. Surely whoever is using the bathroom will go into the red-button room… Wrong. Mara walks through the doorway we are hiding next to and walks straight to her bed without seeing us. I push Avra through the door. I am almost through it myself when I hear Mara say, "Elira, what are you doing in here?"

"I-I have to go to the bathroom. Oops, wrong room. Sorry." I leave the room then run into the bathroom. Avra is standing in front of the laundry chute looking into the chasm and frowning.

"Elira, I don't want to go in there."

"I know, but it's the only way. Now get your legs in there!" I hold Avra's hands as she puts her legs in the chute one at a time. Her whining and moaning aren't helping either of us. "Shh! Now go!" I shove her head the rest of the way in. I hear a small squeal as she disappears from sight.

Loud footsteps and arguing outside the bathroom warn me that I must move now. It sounds like Mara, Shasta, and Mentor Roberta are all trying to talk at once. Oh no! I get my right leg in the laundry chute, then my left leg. I didn't realize that all the layers of clothing I am wearing would bulk me up this much. I should have stopped with two. My hips don't want to slip through... The door opens as I get my hips to pop through the opening, and the last thing I see as my head disappears down the chute is Mara glaring and pointing at me and Mentor Roberta yelling, "Stop!"

Thud. I land in the hamper on a lumpy pile of dirty clothes. I feel big hands on my arms. Garth and Jefrey lift me out of the hamper. We're all there, and the two cutest boys in the complex are touching me at the same time. Ahh! I've got to keep my head in the game. Mentor Roberta will be here in a matter of minutes.

"What kept you? We've been waiting for 10 minutes, Elira." Rocky says to me as I peel my eyes off the twins.

I point across the laundry room. "That way, go!" I take Avra's Scott-free hand and start marching to the other side of the vast laundry room. Everyone follows me at a fast walk.

"Someone was in the bathroom with the laundry chute. They saw me, and now Mentor Roberta is on her way. We have to get out of here now!"

Jefrey starts lashing out. "I knew it. This was such a bad idea. I landed in barf. Now they will catch us and charge us as dissidents. They'll send us to the death doctor..."

Rocky pushes Jefrey from behind. "Shut up, Jefrey, and move faster."

We reach the garbage chute. The opening is twice as big as the laundry chute, thank goodness. The door and its locking mechanism are rather stiff, and the boys have to help me get it open.

Jefrey lifts the black flap in the hole. "There might be barf again."

"Shut up, Jefrey, and go through!" Rocky yells. Jefrey goes through with a helpful shove from his brother.

"Stop, you dissidents!" I hear Mentor Roberta scream as she enters the far end of the laundry room. Mentor Briggs is right behind her. They run toward us. I should have poured a glass of water on Mentor Roberta's communication box today...

Rocky sees the mentors running for us and fills with

adrenalin. He picks Avra up and throws her through the hole, then does the same thing to Scott. Garth resists. "No, Elira first." But Rocky is too strong for Garth. He picks him up like he's a sack of laundry and chucks him through the hole. I push all the wheeled laundry tubs that I can reach into a blockade to slow down the mentors. Rocky is inside the garbage chute with his hands reaching out to me as the mentors push the last laundry tub out of the way. I jump into Rocky's arms and immediately feel gravity pulling us down, Rocky's feet first, but my head first. The smell of rotting garbage we're about to land in fills my nose. My mind screams, *I can't believe it.* We're going to make it,' when something snags my foot. I look back and see Mentor Briggs holding my foot with both hands.

Oh no. Mentor Briggs has a strong grip. I may not make it! But the rest of them can. I look at Rocky and say, "Take care of Avra for me, and tell your mother thank you. Get them away from here now." I let go of him. His face is frozen in horror as he falls.

"No!" he screams, as he lands in the garbage truck.

I look up at Mentor Briggs and my captured foot. I kick, wiggle and flail as hard as I can. My shoe starts to slip off. He calls me an ugly word as my shoe comes off in his hand. The other hand grabs my foot, but all he gets are toes. I feel a crack. This must be a crazy, adrenaline-filled idea, but if I kick really hard, I'll probably break a couple of toes, but I'll get away. It's not even a choice. I kick as hard as I can. I feel the bones of my toes separate from the rest of my foot. Mentor Briggs flinches, loses his grip, and I start to fall again.

Thud. Pain shoots through my neck and foot as I land on a pile of rotten food. My head is dizzy, and my vision is fuzzy.

Mentor Roberta's loud voice rings out into the night as she calls for help into her communication box. "All complex guards run to the garbage truck immediately. Six dissidents are trying to escape!" I really should have ruined her communication box.

"Elira, we have to go! Come on!" I hear Garth's voice yelling at me as I try to stand up. He is the only one left in the truck. He takes my hand, leads me to the side of the truck, picks me up, and throws me over the edge. Jefrey, Scott, and Rocky have formed a human net that catches me. Garth hurls himself over the edge and lands on his feet.

I try to get my head to clear. "We have to get through the trees. Break the branches if you have to. Ernestine is on the other side."

"There they are. Get them!" Mentor Roberta's voice howls. Complex guards are running around both sides of the building, and the trees are still far away. My breath keeps catching in my throat as I run on broken toes. Oh no. They are going to get us.

Rocky yells, "Faster!"

Everyone starts running for their lives. Everyone except me. I can't run as fast as the rest of them can, my toes hurt so bad. Garth turns his head around and sees me struggling. He turns the rest of his body around, picks me up like I'm a baby, and runs for the trees. The guards are right behind us. As we burst through the trees, we see a big wheeled, thing. I want to say it's called a van. I've seen one in a book before. The side door is open, and our friends are inside beckoning us to hurry.

Garth is panting and sweating, but he doesn't slow down. *Bang.* "Uh." Garth stumbles. A guard shot Garth in the ear with something. Blood is running down the side of his face. I close my eyes and start to cry. We're done for.

Suddenly I'm flying through the air. Is this how a bird feels when it flies through the sky? How is this happening? I land inside the van. Garth must have thrown me in. Hands grab me and pull me back. A guard reaches out to grab Garth's shoulder right as he jumps into the van. Ernestine is at the wheel and she takes off with the door still open. Rocky tries to close it as we hear loud shots hitting the van. She doesn't slow down. The farther down the road we get, the quieter the shots get. Rocky gets the door shut and collapses on the middle seat. His voice is quiet, but he says out loud what the rest of us are thinking, "We made it. I can't believe it."

Ernestine's rough alto voice laughs out loud and turns around to look at us. "Congratulations. You're free."

Chapter 27

AVRA LAYS HER HEAD ON SCOTT'S SHOULDER and holds his hand. She is trembling, but she's not crying. I wish I could say the same for myself. Scott seems to be in shock. He's not moving and is staring straight ahead. None of us has ever seen such violence before. Now we are bumping along in some kind of vehicle, which we've never done before either.

Jefrey looks at me and shakes his head. He is still upset that we decided to escape. I wish he wasn't so handsome. It would make it easier to be mad at him.

I take a few deep breaths and wipe the tears from my eyes.

"Do you feel toxins from the earth creeping into your body, Jefrey?" I ask as sarcastically as a bawl baby can.

He frowns at me. "Not the toxins I thought were out here. But I have never been so filthy and lucky to be alive in my life."

I look at Garth. He is biting his lip and holding his hand over his ear. I take his hand off and look at it. Half of his ear has been blown off.

Rocky points to his own deformed lack-of-ear. "It looks like you're my twin now, Garth."

Garth forces a smile on his bloody face for his friend. "Yeah. They'll never be able to tell us apart."

Jefrey smiles at Garth for the first time all day. "I guess we're not identical anymore."

I pull the sock off my shoeless foot and press the cleanest part of the fabric to Garth's ear. He shakes his head and tries to pull it off. "No, Elira. You need it for your foot. You have no shoe, and your toes—they look broken."

I sit up straighter and grimace as I look at them. They are already turning dark and swelling. "Yeah, they are broken. It was either let the toes break and be free, or let them take me back to their pink trays and death doctor. I chose to be free."

Jefrey wipes the crusty tears off my cheek with his hand and shakes his head again. Garth uses his free hand to pick up my broken-toed foot. He just holds it below the toe line in his warm hand. His warmth feels so good on my cold foot. I can't help myself; I start to cry again. I am so relieved we made it, and

I'm hurting so badly at the same time. I lay my head on Garth's shoulder, blood and all. He quietly tells me, "It will be okay," as I cry.

Jefrey looks at me laying against Garth's shoulder, grabs one of my hands, and rubs it gently. He looks at Ernestine. "Hey, I don't know your name, but where exactly are we going?"

"I'm Ernestine, Rocky's mom. We're going to my house for now. Don't worry, I have everything prepared for you. You will ask yourselves why you didn't escape earlier when we get to where we're going."

"I highly doubt that," Jefrey mumbles as he closes his eyes and leans against the van window.

Ernestine keeps looking in the rear-view mirror at us all, or maybe it's just Rocky she's looking at. She clears her throat. "Rocky, climb up here and sit by me, son." She starts to choke up. "I want to look at you. I-I haven't seen you in fourteen years."

Rocky climbs through the tangle of bodies and sits in the seat next to his mother in the front. "So, you are my mother." Ernestine smiles at him and nods. "Where is my father?"

"He is—not here. He is alive, but he's not here. It's a long story."

Rocky turns his head so he can listen with his good ear. "Why did you let them take me, mother? That place is horrible. No one deserves to be there."

Ernestine's eyes fill with agony. She reaches out and takes

239

Rocky's hand. "I didn't let them. I didn't have a choice. When you were born without an inner and outer ear, I knew that the government would take you away from me. I would have you for the first two years, but on January first after you were two, I was required to take you to the ultimate wellness check-up at the city building. Everyone who has a child is required to do so. If you don't show up, like I didn't, armed guards show up at your house to escort you there. The government is determined to get rid of all sickness, deformity, and unattractiveness from the population. So, they take all two-year-olds with any mental or physical problem and stick them in the complex for life."

Rocky looks at his mother and decides to believe her. "Wow. I always wondered. I have a faint memory of you crying and fighting the people who took me away."

"That was the worst day of my life. A government official once told me to be grateful that the problem children of the world go into the complex and cheap goods come out. Society is better for it." She frowns and shakes her head. "It disgusts me. I've been trying everything I can think of for the past 14 years to get you out. I've been put in solitary confinement several times for disturbing the peace. My husband told me I was crazy and left me. But I never gave up!"

Rocky is still medicated, but he recognizes the struggle his mother has had. "Thank you, Mom. I saw you out my window last year several times. I didn't know you were my mother, but I knew from watching you that something wasn't right."

Ernestine nods her head. "I've been hiding in the trees almost every night for the last 14 years, watching the windows for someone to communicate with. It was worth it." Ernestine lets go of Rocky's hand and reaches up to pinch his cheek. "You're even more handsome than I thought you'd be."

Rocky shakes his head and smiles at his mother. "Thanks."

We pull up to a rickety-looking—house, I think. Ernestine pulls the van around back and parks it in an equally rickety-looking little building. We all climb out and watch Ernestine work. She shuts the door to the building she calls "the garage" and latches it.

I look at the bigger building that is kind of like the houses in our text books. "Is this your house?" I ask as I gingerly step on my broken toes. Jefrey looks at the house and scoffs.

"Yes. But we can't stay here. They know I'm Rocky's mother and that I have tried to get him out before. We have to go somewhere they will never look for us. We will have to walk for a while. Is that okay?"

Garth looks at me with inquisitive eyes. "I-I'll be okay." I assure him. My foot is cold and in pain, but I can do this.

We walk on the opposite side of the street of the tall light covered poles that come out of the ground every so often. There is a big, fancy building at the end of the street. We seem to be walking there. I bite my lip. My foot won't stop throbbing. Garth sees me cringing with every step. He picks me up and carries me the rest of the way. I can't look at his bloody ear. I feel personally responsible for it. I lay my head against him and listen to his heart. It is strong and steady, just what I need after a day like this. In fact, the rhythm makes me want to drift off...

When we get to the big fancy building, we walk around the back and down some stairs. Ernestine pushes a button that rings a bell. I want to ask Ernestine what on earth we are doing here, but all I can handle is keeping my sobs of pain inside. So, I just watch things unfold from Garth's arms. Jefrey glares at Garth and then at Ernestine.

"What is this place?"

Ernestine doesn't look worried. "This is the home of my friend. We can trust her."

Jefrey doesn't look convinced. A fancily-dressed woman answers the door. "Get in. Get in!"

We hurry inside. Garth sets me on my own feet. I worry that my dirty feet will stain the beautiful soft flooring. The door clicks shut behind us. We stand there gaping at the beautifully decorated room. Judging from Ernestine's rickety house, this woman must be rich. Why is she helping us?

The fancy woman points to a big black box on a table thing. "You are on the news already. Look!"

We look at the brightly-lit square thing. A fancily-dressed man is sitting behind a desk and saying, "There has been a breakout at the Complex of Undesirables tonight. This is the first recorded breakout in 40 years. If anyone has seen six unappealing individuals wearing jumpsuits this evening, you are asked to contact the authorities. The individual named Ernestine Moore is also wanted for questioning as she has a record of disturbing the peace and is the mother of one of the aforementioned individuals. Now, on to weather..." The lady points a small black box at the big lit-up box and it goes dark.

The fancy lady slowly inches her way toward me. She studies my face with a strange look in her eyes. She reaches out and touches the purple birthmark on the side of my head. I flinch and take a step back, looking at her questioningly. She pretends like my standoffishness doesn't bother her. I pull some hair forward to cover my purple eye as much as possible.

"I wish my husband was here. He is a doctor and he could fix your wounds. But he will not be back until tomorrow. I have rags and disinfectant we can use to clean you up. That is the best we can do until he returns. Any other doctor will turn you in."

Avra starts to whimper. Scott moves her to a chair next to the big, beautiful table on our right and sits down with her. Rocky tries to hide behind his mother, but she takes his hand and pulls him so he is side-by-side with her. Jefrey sits next to Scott at the table and watches the fancy lady with distrust.

Garth pulls his hand off his ear. The blood is making his fingers stick together. He forces his fingers apart. The woman walks over to the sink behind the fancy table and wets a towel. She pulls a box out of a cupboard with some doctor-looking things in it and sets it on the table. She hands Garth the wet towel.

He nods his head in appreciation. "Thank you." I take the wet towel and wash Garth's hand and face for him. It's the least I can do after he saved my life tonight.

The fancy lady looks at us all with compassion. "It looks like none of you will be able to show your faces outside for quite some time. Luckily, there is plenty of room for you all here in the basement. There are three bedrooms down here. One is... for the girls. One is for the boys, and one is for Ernestine."

The lady walks to the left and beckons us to join her. "There is also a hidden room that can be accessed by pulling the red book on this bookshelf." The fancy lady walks straight to a bookshelf that reaches from floor to ceiling and pulls a red book almost off the shelf. We hear a *click*, and the shelf swings forward. A midsized room with three sets of bunk beds around the walls and two sofas facing each other in the middle greet us all. "If the house is ever searched, you must hide in here. You will be able to go outside from time to time though. I will tell the neighbors that you are my hired help."

Why would this fancy woman risk so much for us? I can go no longer without asking, "Who are you?"

The lady takes a step toward me. "Ernestine and I met fourteen years ago. The day that the government took our beautiful babies from us. We were both distraught and tried to comfort each other. Ernestine said she would not rest until she had her son back. She quit her job, which caused financial hardship for her family. I felt terrible about that. So I hired her to investigate the complex to find a way to get our children back. I've been preparing this house to keep our children safe from the government as soon as we could free them. That day has finally come. It's truly a miracle."

She still hasn't answered my question. So I ask again, "What is your name?"

"My name is Florence. Florence Elira Hamble."

About the Author

Heather Hayes loves a good story. She believes a good story will entertain you and leave you feeling like a better person for having read it. She loves living in Idaho with her husband and five daughters. If she isn't writing, she is probably watching a volleyball game, cooking, skiing, reading, or planning a trip to somewhere new.

A Message from Heather Hayes

*If you liked discovering the secrets of the complex with Elira,
please tell your friends about it and leave a review on Amazon; it
helps me out more than you know. The rest of
THE COMPLEX TRILOGY is coming soon to Amazon and
HeatherHayesAuthor.com.*

The Complex Life

The Complex Law (October 2018)

The Complex Leader (November 2018)

*If you like a good story for younger readers, check out my other
books:*

Unexpected Magic

A Tale of Regrets

Rissy's Summer Son

The Fantastic Backyard of Imagination